With Fate
Conspire

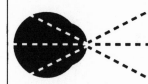

This Large Print Book carries the
Seal of Approval of N.A.V.H.

With Fate Conspire

Yvonne MacManus

Thorndike Press • Thorndike, Maine

Published in 1998 by arrangement with Yvonne MacManus.

Thorndike Large Print ® Candlelight Series.

The tree indicium is a trademark of Thorndike Press.

The text of this Large Print edition is unabridged.
Other aspects of the book may vary from the original edition.

Set in 16 pt. Plantin by Minnie B. Raven.

Printed in the United States on permanent paper.

Library of Congress Cataloging in Publication Data

MacManus, Yvonne.
    With fate conspire / Yvonne MacManus.
        p.   cm.
    ISBN 0-7862-1430-9 (lg. print : hc : alk. paper)
    1. Large type books.   I. Title.
    [PS3563.A31885W5   1998]
    813´.54—dc21   98-5563

For R.J.A.P. and
Kubi-Chan

Ah Love! could thou and I with Fate
  conspire
To grasp this sorry Scheme of Things
  entire,
Would not we shatter it to bits — and
  then
Re-mould it nearer to the Heart's Desire!
— *Rubaiyat of Omar Khayyam, LXXIII,*
  translated by Edward Fitzgerald

Chapter 1

With a lumbering tenacity, fog devoured the verdant mountains that rose sharply to the east of the Pacific; the ocean itself, alternately reflecting the gray above it and the brilliant blues and greens of direct sunlight upon its oblivious waters, gently caressed jagged reefs and smooth but monstrous boulders. Jeannine Wellman absorbed the view in humble yet proud silence. Though awed by the enormity and beauty of nature untrampled by man, she was also keenly aware that only man could relate to such a vista with an emotional and intellectual respect.

To her right, as far as she could see, every imaginable shade of green was represented in the rolling hills and sharp mountains. Occasionally, a rooftop could be discerned; here a fence; there a glimpse of a road with a fleck of a car seen rounding a sharp curve; and spotted across the lower slopes were patches of what Jeannine assumed to be heather — patchwork reliefs of violet nestled in the predominant green. With a nearly religious sense of exaltation, she twisted in her seat to peer toward the west, past the immediate natural fence of fir trees girdling the rocky beaches to the sea beyond.

She longed to be alone, walking privately in physical communication with nature's eloquence, and her imagination briefly toyed with a child's possessive wish to be all alone upon the earth, to be the sole inhabitant amidst such spectacular and dramatic beauty; but the thought was swiftly broken. Even as the Greyhound shifted into a lower gear, groaning up the steep grade of Highway 1, Jeannine's fellow passengers oohed and ahhed amongst themselves, fumbling with cameras of every description, blocking the windows by holding up disinterested infants to face the view, thus converting moments of breathtaking sanctity into loud enthusiasms. She was sure her co-passengers would have had the same reactions to the Haunted House ride in Disneyland.

Jeannine Wellman was again made deeply aware of how different she was from her average fellow human beings. They were enjoying themselves, and blissfully unaware of how their easy enthusiasm forced Jeannine into deeper and deeper isolated introspection. She envied these Other People. At twenty-seven, she had yet to learn how to show emotion, how to merely let go and be herself. She had learned how to cope with others; how to "handle" people or difficult situations; and she appeared to do both quite well. In fact, there was only one person in the world who knew and understood her facades: her dear friend and personal physician, Dr. Vincent Sternig. And it was the good doctor who had given her the ultimatum that caused her now to be on her way to Carmel, California, on board a crowded Greyhound bus filled with summer tourists and their progeny. Her last attack had been quite serious; that, coupled with the constant tensions of her job, had made Dr. Sternig warn her: "If you don't get the hell out of this smog, out of that nervous breakdown you call a job . . . I wouldn't give you any odds on your life. These pressures will only bring on more attacks in your rundown condition, and your heart cannot survive many more."

His words had had the desired effect. Jeannine had done many foolish things in her life, usually from a gullible trust, but she was not suicidal. Now, four weeks later, she was on her way to Carmel-by-the-Sea: pronounced by its Chamber of Commerce *the* Village of Romance; denounced by outsiders as an overpriced and overrated tourist trap; and protected and smothered with incestuous love by its regular inhabitants, who would not alter one grain of sand or shift one leaf.

She had resolved that if she had to give up everything she had worked for, she would only make the sacrifice if she could live near the sea. But not many people are wealthy enough to require the services of a personal secretary, especially one who wanted to live upon the premises, near to the sea. There were job opportunities in San Francisco, San Diego, even in Monterey — but she quickly dismissed them when she saw she would be trading one set of pressures for another. No. It had to be remote but not distant; quiet but not entombed. When Dr. Sternig told her of the position open at Carmel — one that he'd heard about from another patient — she wrote immediately to the prospective employer. It was a very awkward letter to write since she knew so little about the requirements, or even, for that matter, if the position was still available. But Dr. Sternig encouraged her, reminding her that all she could lose was a ten-cent stamp, and that anyone would be damned lucky to get a girl with her qualifications. Jeannine laughed and replied that she would be sure to include in her letter that she was a secretary without peer — provided she was well enough to come to work.

The application letter was formal, yet cordial. Keeping the letter very simple and to the point, she asked if the position was still available, what the duties, requirements and salary were, and said that she would be pleased to submit a resume for consideration. It was neatly typed on Dr. Sternig's office Selectric, and signed with her own unforgettable signature, which proclaimed her existence with an individualistic flourish. She paused briefly to be sure she had not misspelled anything on the envelope:

> Mrs. Josefina de Lorca
> "Puerta de Paz"
> Paseo Cabrillo
> Carmel-by-the-Sea, California

Just the address was so romantic that Jeannine dropped the white envelope into the mailbox with higher hopes than it was wise to entertain. Yet within a week she received a reply — two parchment stationery pages, written in a formal European hand, and in real ink. The contents were neither cordial nor rude, but a simply stated reply to the questions posed. The duties involved those of a social secretary, and since Mrs. de Lorca was involved in local ecological conservation groups, organizational abilities were necessary as well as an ability to get along with members of committees; a good mind for detail; at least average shorthand skills; she should be personable and well-bred; a positive but not aggressive personality; and it would be necessary for the applicant to live at "Puerta de Paz" rather than in town, since the hours were irregular, and, on occasion, when there was no one else at the house, Mrs. de Lorca wanted someone with her at all times, since she suffered from arthritis of the knees. And — this struck Jeannine as a bit eccentric — would Miss Wellman kindly send her reply in her own handwriting rather than use a typewriter.

So, on this perfect day, the 15th of April, 1974, four weeks later, Jeannine Wellman was to begin her new life. She felt that her decision to leave Los Angeles behind was a wise one. It occurred to her that she might hate Mrs. de Lorca, loathe "Puerta de Paz," despise the nature of her duties; but she had only to remind herself that she was not leaving the country nor going to Mars, that if she didn't like it there, she could . . . she could . . . What *could* she do if she didn't like it? she asked herself silently as the bus began its downhill descent toward the Monterey depot.

There's not even a bus stop in Carmel, she thought wryly. And the familiar sensation of lack of sufficient air began to flush her otherwise pale cheeks, the increased pulse rate, the light but telltale hammering of her heart within her breast, the shallow rapid breaths. This is ridiculous, she told herself severely, I'm not a child, afraid of the unknown and the dark.

By the time the bus reached the depot, and the other passengers were busily gathering belongings and donning sweaters, Jeannine had regained her composure.

"Here we are, folks, beautiful downtown Monterey. Have a nice time!" The driver looked at his watch, then up toward the darkening sky, and winked playfully at Jeannine as she followed the gaily clad vacationers off the bus.

The acrid smell of carbon monoxide and exhaust fumes blended nauseatingly with the aromas of a nearby snack stand and mixed with the wafting colors of the conflicting perfumes, colognes, and shaving lotions of the milling passengers embarking and disembarking at the depot. For a moment, Jeannine did indeed feel very much like a child, as if she should have her name and destination pinned to her coat lapel. She had been instructed to wait at the ticket counter, where Mrs. de Lorca's driver, Manuel, would present himself and drive her to "Puerta de Paz." Rooted to the spot for over ten minutes, she had been eyed with curiosity by a couple of sailors, scrutinized shrewdly by a policeman, asked by an old lady if she knew where the rest rooms were, and foully breathed upon by a middle-aged tourist suggesting that she join him for a drink.

Her mind raced with possibilities, most of them unpleasant. Mrs. de Lorca had forgotten about her arrival; worse, she had changed her mind about hiring her and planned to leave her standing there for as long as she was foolish enough to do so. Manuel had gone over a cliff. Mrs. de Lorca had fallen suddenly ill and had been unable to dispatch Manuel. These, and many more frustrating alternatives flashed through Jeannine's head. She had just decided to give Manuel five more minutes before telephoning the house, when a short and very dapper man of indeterminate age approached her.

Dressed in a dark suit, only his cap gave clue to his profession — a cap which he doffed as he approached her.

"Señorita Wellman?"

Jeannine's smile was one of genuine relief, verging on gratitude. "Manuel?"

"Please? You follow me for me to take you to the hacienda?" Deftly, the wiry chauffeur picked up her two suitcases and her overnight case and began to lead the way out of the depot. Once outside, he paused only long enough to open the door to the black Cadillac, circa 1950, closed the door, and then went to the rear of the automobile to place her luggage in the trunk. During the brief wait, Jeannine saw that downtown Monterey was a rather dreary place, with its brightly neoned bars and abundance of cheap hotels. Though the evening was chilly, no one seemed to be wearing an overcoat. As Manuel situated himself behind the driving wheel, Jeannine realized that she was completely separated from him by a solid sheet of thick glass. Glancing about the perfectly kept interior of the back seat, she noted the horn of the intercom system affixed to the doorpost on her right. If the car had been sealed in an airtight compartment since 1950, it couldn't have been in more perfect condition. Jeannine won-

15

dered if, perhaps, there was some deep, dark family secret; some horrible event that had occurred at "Puerta de Paz" over twenty years ago that had stilled any desire to remain in the present — if, maybe, all the clocks at the house would be stopped at the same time. But she smiled to herself immediately at her own dramatic fantasies. Mrs. de Lorca was probably a devastatingly handsome woman in her late fifties, clad in a Jax pants suit — but no, that image simply didn't fit the known facts. The formal letters, the incapacity occasionally imposed by arthritis, the isolation of the house itself . . . these things did not add up to a sophisticated, chic older woman, and neither did the vintage limousine. The bubble picturing charming, intimate parties, rides through the countryside with extravagant brunches afterward, faded then dissolved with pathetic ease. In its place rose visions of dark, dank halls, ancestral portraits with eyes that followed you wherever you went, a house that creaked strangely in the night. . . .

From time to time, Manuel twisted in his seat and smiled at Jeannine through the glass; a smile that shyly suggested that he understood her apprehensions and that she need not feel all alone in the world. And as the car sped onto Highway 1, leaving behind the garish glitter of downtown Monterey, the stillness and the night conspired to defeat Manuel's reassurances. Only the highway itself seemed of this world, seemed real. Around them there was nothing but a kind of undulating blackness that made the dashboard lights seem too bright, and the headlights ineffectual beacons into the void. As the large limousine solemnly progressed around curves, over and down hills, Jeannine would catch a glimpse of lights within a home off in the distance, but soon even that comfort was denied her. The highway became surrounded with thick brush and trees, which muffled the sound of the engine; and as if a layer of gray gauze had been dropped directly in front of the hood, the car seemed to be suddenly surrounded by a distorting fog that converted the formerly brilliant incision of the headlights into a rather diffused, jaundiced glow.

Manuel turned again, and though Jeannine knew he meant to smile at her again, she could barely make out his face; and it seemed, for a split second, that he had more teeth than a human being should have; and she instantly berated herself for such childishness. Instead, she concentrated on forcing herself to treat this entire excursion as a marvelous adventure, not dangerous, per-

17

haps, but certainly exciting — and something that she would joke about in the months to come when she and Mrs. de Lorca became very good friends.

A dull blood-red glow hung above them unexpectedly, and Manuel brought the Cadillac to a halt. Jeannine laughed aloud and whispered to herself, "Where there be traffic lights, there be no vampires!"

Then Manuel turned off the main road, and again there was only the night, the interior of the car, and her imagination.

Chapter 2

"Aquí estamos," Manuel confided as he walked briskly ahead of her up the field-stone stairs to the broad veranda of the house. It seemed to Jeannine that it had taken hours to reach the estate — or the hacienda, as Manuel insisted — and she was sure that the drive could not possibly have been as treacherous as her night-induced fears envisioned. An elaborate wrought-iron coach lamp illuminated a massive scrolled oak door. There was a heavy iron door-knocker, but Manuel pushed the button for the gonglike chimes instead — smiling and whispering that soon she would be inside the warm hacienda, comfortable, and with *la señora.*

Jeannine wondered why he felt it necessary to whisper, and then realized that she, too, had been whispering since the car had pulled up on the circular gravel driveway. The crunching noise of the tires upon the pebbles had seemed ear-splitting, and once she was out of the car, Jeannine had felt overwhelmed with the silence. And yet, there was sound. Unaccustomed sounds. As she felt the sea breeze curiously investigate her auburn hair, smelled the sharp saltiness of the air, felt the damp upon her face, she realized that the sounds were those of leaves brushing against one another, breaking the silence with a night-obscured softshoe dance of communication. A low, occasional rumble gradually broke into her awareness, and only by its rhythm did she know that it had to be the waves far below them. She knew that the house must be located quite high, since her ears had popped on the drive up; and that knowledge served to heighten her appreciation of the quiet — otherwise, she could never have heard the ocean from so great a distance.

Even before the massive door opened, Jeannine was sure she would love the house, love living there. She had no way of knowing just exactly where she was, or what direction they faced, or even if the door opened into a cave; but the peace, the stillness, the vitality of nature near an ocean, these gave her poise. After living in Los Angeles, with the noise and the traffic at all hours, she felt transported to another world, a world where time stood still; where taming a bird would be cruel, and taking a snapshot ludicrous. Despite her qualms about meeting Mrs. de Lorca, Jeannine was strangely collected; no one surrounded by such serenity could possibly be irrational or formidable.

Suddenly she found herself, and Manuel, bathed in a richly warm shaft of light as the front door opened. A short, rotund woman, whose tanned skin breached no wrinkle, and whose long black hair was worn in a simple, neat bun at the nape of her short neck, greeted them.

"Ay, es la señorita Wellman, sí? Pase, pase, señorita, bienvenida . . ." She curtsied awkwardly, wiping her hands on the coarse linen apron she wore over a full-length bright-green skirt. *"La señora le espera,"* she said, then grinned and playfully slapped her own mouth. "The señora, she is waiting for you," she translated, then she lightly boxed Manuel on the ear. "You! What took you so long? If you stopped at the cantina, la señora will . . ."

"Por favor, Chata! Please! It was the fog. I stopped nowhere. Is that not correct, señorita?"

Jeannine smiled and decided that mentioning he was a little late in picking her up would not serve the purpose of household harmony.

"My wife, señorita Wellman, Chata.

21

That's her how-you-say, her —"

"Nickname," Jeannine volunteered.

"Sí, sí. It means someone with a very short nose, but Chata, she is short all over. Yes? But she is a good woman, señorita, and a very good cook, too." Manuel paused in his praise to scowl at the woman. *"Anda! Vete! Lleva estas maletas a su cuarto — aspúrate!"*

While the domestic orders were being given, Jeannine began to take in the foyer. It was a magnificent, spacious adobe hacienda, the kind one read about or saw in home-decorating magazines; dark-red tile floor with scattered and well-worn oriental rugs, and commanding, heavy antique tables or small chests wherever there was enough wall space to accommodate them. Jeannine was pleased to see that the furniture was of European origin and not the ubiquitous imitation Spanish Mediterranean that had swept good taste into a potpourri of conformity. Overhead were exposed mahogany beams; to her left, a broad tile stairway with iron railing; and to her right, large double doors. Directly ahead of her was a stained-glass round window, recessed at least a foot into the adobe wall, and a doorway that she guessed would lead to the kitchen and the servants' quarters. She was

22

amused, and relieved, that there was not a family portrait to be seen.

Manuel helped Chata pick up the suitcases, watched her lumber up the stairway with them, then turned to Jeannine. "Please? Follow me?"

He walked the few steps to the double doors, rapped lightly, then opened them, standing to one side to allow Jeannine to pass. As she entered, she couldn't prevent the gasp of surprise that escaped her lips. It was the most incredibly beautiful room she had ever seen. Tastefully opulent, it had to measure at least fifty by fifty feet, she estimated. Mammoth tapestries hung from two walls, sconces made from iron and amber listed safely at fifteen-foot intervals, framing a walk-in fireplace and various paintings — Jeannine was certain that at least three Cézannes and two Turners were to her left. Deep plush divans seemed to swim in the expanse of the room, surrounded by clusters of low armchairs; fruitwood and pecan end tables lent convenience, and a round Oriental teakwood coffee table dominated one seating cluster, while another was serviced by an imposing Jacobean oak table with Tudor rose carvings; two Empire sofas rested snugly against opposite walls. But what took Jeannine's imagination and held it fast was the wall she faced upon entering. Fifty feet of patio glass doors supported by adobe arches, leading to a broad balcony. Jeannine needed no daylight to tell her of the view it would command. It was a room belonging to someone of many and varied tastes . . . all of them indulgent, but exquisite. Instead of clashing for attention, jumbling the senses with too many impressions, each unique piece blended into a rich, harmonious whole as rewarding as a final chord by Beethoven. And one simply knew that from here there could only flow grace and dignity and a great sense of inner calm. There was nothing to do, after being in that room, but to possess it or feel forever cheated.

And it was with a very guilty start that Jeannine realized she'd been addressed. She turned, blushing slightly, toward the sound of the voice.

"You find the room to your satisfaction, Miss Wellman?"

The room had seemed so empty, so devoid of any presence other than her own, that Jeannine had a moment's difficulty locating Mrs. de Lorca. Seated but a scant ten feet away, dressed in heavy black lace from throat to ankles, was Mrs. de Lorca. She rose slowly, laboriously, and with obvious effort crossed to where Jeannine stood. Slightly stooped, but with her head high, the ancient woman approached the rooted girl and stood at least five inches beneath Jeannine's five-foot-six height. "It's a very, very old room, Miss Wellman," she said with a clear contralto voice, "but then, so am I . . . so am I. Won't you be seated?"

With some force of will, Jeannine pulled her gaze away frown the old woman's eyes, away from their lama's cognizance, their Krishna's acceptance. Jeannine had assumed that Mrs. de Lorca would be a mature woman; even elderly, perhaps. But the woman she had just met seemed fragile as parchment, ancient as papyrus scrolls, her flesh the stuff of spun cobwebs. Her features were thin, and it took little to see how beautiful she had once been. Her high forehead stretched tautly across a wide brow with a thousand infinitesimal lines; her nose, though slightly aquiline, divided her penetrating eyes with pride and well-deserved arrogance; and her mouth — now thin and devoid of sensuous flesh — was straight, as if she'd long ago decided that an excess of mirth could only lead to an excess of sorrow, and she would bow to neither. A woman of will, rigid in her principles, who rejected benevolence lest it be abused. But

25

those eyes . . . those eyes shamed anyone who had not lived as long and seen so much. Jeannine felt like an awkward school-girl before the headmistress, as she made her way to the divan nearest Mrs. de Lorca, who had carefully seated herself in a high-backed Queen Anne chair.

"Would you care for some sherry? Or perhaps a drink?"

"I-I wouldn't want to be any trouble, Mrs. de Lorca," she began hesitantly, fearing that the sound of her voice might shatter the woman's entire being.

"Don't be silly, child," she replied, and a hint of a smile played across her lips. "I am old . . . but I am not dead." She lifted a cane that she had crooked upon the arm of her chair, and brought it down resoundingly on the tile floor. Manuel entered seconds later, grinning happily.

"I felt that to my toes in the kitchen!" he announced with pride.

"Manuel, give Miss Wellman a drink. What will it be, some Scotch, perhaps? Come, come! At my age, I can't waste time waiting for people to make up their minds!"

"S-scotch would be fine," Jeannine answered.

"How long have you had that speech impediment?"

"What speech impediment?" Jeannine asked, her color rising.

"My dear child, this is not Shangri-la and I am not Father Perrault. If I'd wanted reverence in a secretary, I would have trained a dog to type!"

As if she had been slapped from a stupor, Jeannine found her tongue and her spine simultaneously. "Manuel, I'd far prefer a vodka martini . . . with a lemon twist."

The old woman nodded slowly. "Well, I'm glad that's out of the way. Now we can talk seriously. Manuel, I'll have the usual."

Jeannine watched as Manuel crossed to a sideboard and proceeded to pour three fingers of Rémy Martin into a snifter, then bring it to Mrs. de Lorca on a Japanese enameled tray. He returned quickly to the sideboard and prepared a small decanter of martinis, placed it, and a glass, on a duplicate tray and brought it to Jeannine, setting it down on the coffee table before her.

"That will be all, Manuel. Miss Wellman can pour for herself."

He bowed slightly, then left the room quietly.

"Here's to us, *niña,* to a long and enjoyable relationship," she said, raising her snifter to the light and then sipping from it sedately.

Jeannine took a long, grateful swallow from her martini without removing her eyes from Mrs. de Lorca. Of all the things her mind had conjured, Mrs. de Lorca had not been among them. Nor had the isolation of the house, nor had that magnificent room been a part. The mere fact that a woman of her age would even require a secretary was incredible; but then, so was the fact that the woman was still so alive — and so beautiful, despite her years.

"Now then, hard as it may be for you to believe, I have a good deal to say about this general area and what happens here. I very rarely leave the house, but when I do, it's an absolute tour of inspection. The City Council trembles, and I'm told that even Sacramento is informed whenever I go into the valley or into Carmel itself. At one time, much of this area belonged to my family and to the family of my husband, along with a few other landed gentry Spanish ancestors. I shan't go into their histories; you can read about them, if you wish, in the Harrison Memorial Library. But right here, right in these Santa Lucia Mountains, this was all ours under a land grant from King Philip III of Spain."

She paused and sipped again. "Am I boring you?"

"On the contrary," Jeannine said sincerely. "I've a lazy mind. I love history, but reading about it puts me to sleep. I love to hear about it, though; it somehow comes alive then."

"I see. *Bueno,* around 1833 this area became the thorn in the Mexican Republic's side. She had taken possession of it, and having severed her relations with Spain, she ordered that all Spanish subjects leave this region. This land had belonged to Spaniards since 1770, and brash young Mexico was going to exercise its newfound authority. Today, of course, the Church is very pacific" — she laughed in a couple of short gasps — "but in the old days, the Church was a tiger. The Franciscan padres were not accustomed to being told what to do by young Mexican officers of the Republic . . . and they had no intention of ever becoming accustomed to it. Sadly, their stubbornness resulted in the lands being confiscated, and, gradually, everything that had been here fell into ruin. The lands went untilled, the mission decayed." Mrs. de Lorca stopped and sighed heavily. "I've not talked this much in quite some time, *niña.* Let me get my breath," she said, and rested her thin head against the back of her chair. "How's your drink? The truth, now!"

"A little heavy on the vermouth," Jeannine said lightly, "but not unbearably so."

"You shall have to teach Manuel how you like them. He's as stubborn as I am, but he's a kind and devoted friend." The aged hand lifted the nearly empty glass, and the bright eyes focussed on Jeannine. "Get me another, child. I need my strength."

"Is it good for you, Mrs. de Lorca?"

"I see," the woman said, a touch of impatience in her voice. "I think it fair to warn you that, while I wish you to be comfortable in my presence, I do not wish to have my orders questioned. Do you suppose for one moment, at my age, that it could possibly matter whether or not brandy is good for me?"

Jeannine repressed a smile. Josefina de Lorca was a fraud. A cantankerous, delightful, stubborn, charming old woman who had long ago learned the value of an austere exterior, but who had never lost her sense of humor. Jeannine went over to the sideboard and poured Mrs. de Lorca another two fingers of brandy . . . and mixed herself another decanter of martinis. If she were going to hear the entire history of the State of California, she'd need them. When she returned to her seat, the old lady was sitting quietly with her eyes closed, her breathing barely visible. But the hand that held the snifter held it securely — if she were dozing, she had learned to do it without spilling a drop.

"Suffice it to say," the woman's deep voice suddenly broke through the room, "that it wasn't until 1883 that this area saw any restoration. There was a long, dreary period of land speculators, and after a while it became a tourist attraction. But its development, as planned by that Yankee Duckworth, never materialized the way he had hoped. To cut a long dry story short, little by little people began to build here, to settle. Carmel, as we know it today, began to take a harmonious form in the twenties; and it was agreed that the native scenic beauty of the area should never be disturbed. That's why you'll find trees in the middle of the street, and our tree-lined sidewalks are famous. We're a community filled with cranks, and we like it that way. We don't believe in numbers on houses, and for years we refused to install electricity — you'd frequently see processions of people with candles seeking their way home on moonless nights after long walks, or gathering firewood, or just visiting with other Carmelites. We still have precious few street lights . . . I'd strongly suggest that you carry a flashlight with you in the evenings, even in the heart of town. But enough of all this . . . you'll soon learn it all on your own anyway."

"Then your secretarial needs are for the work you do to preserve the community?"

"I don't give a damn what they do with the town of Carmel! Bunch of hypocrites and pseudo-intellectuals, the lot of them! No, girl, I care what is happening all around us. To nature. To our woods and valleys, to our coast and mountains. Wherever people go, it's bound to become a hopeless mess. I want to keep people out of here . . . to preserve what nature we have left so that your great-grandchildren will still know what a valley looks like, or a mountain without subdivided housing tracts or hotels . . . what the ocean looks like without an oil derrick in the middle of the view. It's too late for places like Santa Barbara; whether they know it or not, it's downhill now. But I can fight to save my valley, and our magnificent stretch of ocean frontage."

Mrs. de Lorca began coughing fitfully, her anger having reached a dangerous point. Just as Jeannine jumped up to take the glass from her hand, to try to help the woman, the double doors flew open violently. Jeannine turned to see who would have the audacity to enter in that fashion, and was briefly frightened by the scowling, tall figure that stood in the doorway; a big man dressed in a rust-colored sweater and faded denims. A man in his mid-thirties, and a man who bore a startling resemblance to Mrs. de Lorca.

"Who in the hell are you, and what in blazes are you doing here?"

Chapter 3

In the week that followed, Jeannine was to recall her first impression of Miguel de Lorca with a shudder. Had there been a high wind and howling dogs to accentuate his abrupt and threatening entrance into the room, and her thoughts, it would have seemed perfectly natural. His large dark eyes, so like his grandmother's, blazed with a fury that would better befit a thwarted apostle of the Devil; his unruly black hair — reaching just to his collar — seemed carved into a deliberate tousled effect like a da Vinci sculpture; and his tall, strong body moved lithely yet with the surety of someone who has spent a great deal of time at sea — something his deeply tanned hands and face supported as a strong possibility. Had Miguel de Lorca been born to the role of the dark, sinister avenging angel, he could not have been more forcefully convincing than on that first meeting, framed in the doorway, demanding an explanation, and somehow managing by his mere presence to evoke in Jeannine a great sense of unjustified guilt.

He strode past her to his grandmother, taking command instantly. Lifting the frail woman from her high-backed chair, he barked at her to summon Manuel. "Don't block my way, woman. Get Manuel and tell him to call Dr. Ortíz immediately!" He took a few steps toward the double doors, then paused for a fraction of a second to glance back at Jeannine. "Well?"

"I-I'm here as Mrs. de Lorca's . . ."

"I don't give a damn why you're here right now! Do as I've told you!" The old woman began coughing again, and he left.

He disappeared up the broad tile stairway before Jeannine had a chance to collect herself. Her reflexes were momentarily dulled by his effrontery, his unwarranted rudeness. She was not accustomed to being treated that way, or to being spoken to so harshly. At least, not since her childhood, when she'd been orphaned at the age of eight and raised by a resentful, embittered aunt. Rudeness still brought out the worst in Jeannine; caused her to rebel without reason, to become flustered and react with a sense of emotional injury far surpassing the source. A gentle soul, Jeannine Wellman did not understand such people. She had never understood why there were those who felt it necessary to demand when they could request, to command when they need only guide. These people who lived a constant vendetta with life, who seemed propelled by wounds too deep to recall, were aliens to Jeannine. She had spent most of her adult life shunning such people. They frightened her. It was not a physical fear, rather it was something akin to the fear of a dangerous species which, even when in captivity and rendered harmless in a cage, seemed to constitute a threat to her well-arranged docile personality. And while she knew that there were human beings who lived by threat instead of love, such people invariably unnerved her. Miguel de Lorca seemed just such a man.

Shortly after seven in the morning, on her first Saturday at "Puerta de Paz," Jeannine donned a faded pair of jeans, old sneakers — the canvas worn and threadbare — and an impossibly huge man's sweatshirt. She pulled her shoulder-length russet hair into a makeshift ponytail, feeling certain that she would encounter no one at so early an hour. Then she drove the small black VW to the Carmel River Beach area, parked and began to walk along the beach, teasingly out of reach of the gentle, sinuous tongues of the ocean upon the shore. The sun was already high, and the morning's fog was swiftly evaporating. Like the aftermath of a brawling party, the tide had left its revelry's debris upon the sand and Jeannine padded contentedly through the Braille-like patterns of seaweed and soggy branches, twigs, rusted bits of metal no longer identifiable, a dead sea gull half decayed and drydocked flotsam and jetsam.

The early morning sea breeze kissed her scrubbed face with a salty disrespect and managed to invade the fabric of her sweatshirt with a chilling dampness so that she resorted to folding her arms against it. The broad beach, which narrowed to a ribbon on the unsymmetrical shoreline, was punctuated by jutting, imposing rocks and reefs like tropical icebergs warning of dangerous waters. Despite the early hour, Jeannine noted that she was not totally alone on the beach. There were at least two other people to be discerned: a huddled figure in the distance staring out to sea, and nearer to the tree-crowned bluffs someone seemed to be collecting firewood. They were too remote, though, to deprive Jeannine of her sense of isolation from the world. At worst, they merely reminded her of her own humanity and mortality in such a setting of eternal life and regeneration.

Once again she strove to understand what

compelled Mrs. de Lorca's grandson to behave with such unabashed hostility. The physician, Dr. Ortíz — who looked more like a calculating banker than a kindly doctor — had reassured them all that it was nothing, that at Mrs. de Lorca's age any excitement was bound to bring on a physical reaction of one kind or another. He had cautioned them all to keep Mrs. de Lorca inactive and confined to bed for at least one week, that she should not be permitted any exertion — either physical or mental — for that entire period. Jeannine had been somewhat surprised to overhear Dr. Ortíz's comment to Miguel at the great front door just before he'd left.

"I'd love to know just how old la señora really is," Dr. Ortíz sighed as if standing at the foot of the eighth wonder of the world. And Miguel's swift reply: "As old as time itself, and as fleetingly gone."

It had seemed a strange answer, yet it showed another side to the churlish man; a poetic awe that made Jeannine realize there was a camouflaged sensibility within the scowling facade of Miguel de Lorca. Why he chose to protect himself against the world, she didn't know; and, in truth, she knew it was none of her business. She had been hired to work for the old woman, not for the grandson . . . and she must never forget that.

"La señora siente mucho mejor," Manuel said, grinning happily at Jeannine as she let herself into the kitchen an hour later. Chata was busily preparing a breakfast for la señora that Jeannine was certain would be bad for the old woman, but she thought it wiser to say nothing.

"That smells divine, Chata. What on earth are you cooking?" She helped herself to a cup of strong, freshly brewed coffee and sat down at the worn wooden table with Manuel.

"Fried bananas, señorita . . . with *un poco de canela,*" she said, extending the frying pan beneath Jeannine's nose, tempting her with the aroma.

"Is the señora feeling that much better? Well enough for fried foods?" Jeannine kept her voice light so that no possible censure could be implied, nor offense taken.

"You know how she is," Manuel shrugged. "What good is life if one cannot enjoy it? La señora loves her *huevos rancheros* and her cinnamon bananas . . . would you have the heart to tell her no?"

Jeannine laughed, shaking her head with good-natured resignation. "No. I don't suppose I could."

"El señor Miguel, he awaits your company for breakfast, señorita Wellman," Manuel said, his eyes twinkling as he pretended to tug on an imaginary beard, indicating that she should not keep the Big Man waiting.

"I'll run upstairs and change," Jeannine said, helping herself to the *burrito* Manuel had just prepared for himself. "Tell His Highness I won't be a moment."

True to her promise, Jeannine managed to wash, change to a shirtmaker dress that changed the color of her hazel eyes to green, added a little eyebrow pencil and a light shade of lipstick, and sauntered — as casually as she could muster — down the stairway to the dining room. She was somewhat surprised to find that Miguel was not there, and that the massive oak table was not set for breakfast. Manuel stuck his head through the swinging door and silently gestured to her that "Don Miguel" was out on the balcony off the living room. She nodded, and walked across the wide hall, her leather heels making a dull clicking sound, and into the *sala*. The room still overwhelmed her, still made her painfully aware of her own humble origins, but the sight of Miguel standing on the balcony directly ahead of her forced all other thoughts from her head except her nagging fear of him. Though his broad back was to her, she could tell that he was holding something as he gazed out to the west — probably something as lethal as a cup of coffee, she chided herself, and she vowed not to let her fear of him show.

"Ah, Miss Wellman, do join me," Miguel said, turning at the sound of her footsteps. "It is time that we get to know each other a little better." His eyes seemed less scrutinizing in the sunlight, his expression less threatening amidst the postcard beauty of carefully tended azaleas, cerulean ocean and bright sky. Miguel held the wrought-iron patio chair for her, indicating with a nod of his handsome but guarded face that everything was in readiness for their breakfast.

Though he hadn't said so, Jeannine couldn't help feeling that there was just a hint of disapproval at her tardiness. Nothing specific, nothing tangible, yet . . . And she wondered what had ever happened to the self-assured executive secretary she had been only a week before; to the confident and socially proper woman she had learned to become before she'd quit her job. As Brick Putnam's right hand, she had assisted him in all his wheeling and dealing with movie moguls and dilettante financiers.

41

Seven days before, she knew what made the world go around and what people sought from it: fame, power, and quick riches — usually in that order. But on that balcony, with the Carmel Valley below her and the village huddling at the ocean's edge, in the presence of Miguel de Lorca, she was once again an orphaned little girl — angry with herself for feeling so terribly vulnerable, and angrier still with him for making her feel that way.

"Coffee?" he asked softly, already pouring it.

"Thank you," Jeannine said, cursing the near-whisper in her voice. She watched the man as he replaced the carafe on its stand, his strong, big-boned hands effortlessly transporting it, admired his graceful masculinity as he took the chair opposite her. Not entirely sure of herself, she lifted the cup of steaming coffee to her lips. This is ridiculous, she told herself. Shape up, Jeannine Wellman — there's no callboard for Jane Eyres this year!

"You're smiling, Miss Wellman, I'm glad," Miguel said, breaking into her thoughts. "I had hoped we'd have an opportunity before this to talk, but . . ."

Jeannine suddenly realized that he too felt a discomfort with their first real meeting,

42

and she was not above a slightly sadistic sense of triumph. "It's been hectic settling into my duties, and of course, Mrs. de Lorca's illness has complicated matters." She didn't bother to mention his aloofness, the hours he spent shut up in the study — and she certainly didn't feel it was her place to indicate her awareness of the fact that he would leave his room during the middle of the night, and not return until dawn. She had not been hired as his chaperone and, curious as she was, she had an enormous respect for the privacy of others.

"Yes, that's true," Miguel said, as a charmingly boyish smile played on his lips, "but I've been very remiss, I fear. Especially since my grandmother has not been well, I should have made more of an effort before today."

Jeannine could hardly argue with that since it echoed her own feelings, so she returned his smile — graciously forgiving, she hoped — but said nothing. Fortunately, Chata appeared at that moment, followed by Manuel pushing a sideboard cart with their breakfast. Jeannine was pleased to see that they would enjoy the same fare as Mrs. de Lorca, and when Chata set the steaming bowl of *frijoles* on the table, Jeannine couldn't prevent a gasp of delight.

Miguel chortled. "You seem surprised at our menu, Miss Wellman."

She inclined her head in slight embarrassment. "I didn't know that the Spanish ate Mexican food," she explained.

"Why not?" he asked directly and simply. "You're being very gringo, you know. Are you surprised to see Americans eating Italian food? Or Chinese? Do you think only Americans eat the foods of other countries?" His deep voice held a trace of good-natured mockery.

"I-I frankly never really thought about it," she replied and for the hundredth time since her arrival at Paz wondered where in the world she'd developed a stammer — she'd never had one before, that she could remember. There was definitely something about the de Lorca family and their home that made her feel terribly ill at ease and unsure of herself; and since Jeannine was not given to elaborate rationalizations, she knew that it was her own sense of inadequacy that was bringing it on, and not anything that either of the de Lorcas had done or said — except, perhaps, for that first meeting with Miguel.

"And besides," he continued, ladling out an enormous portion of *frijoles*, "most of us have a strong identification with Mexico.

While our blood may be Spanish, we are culturally closer to Mexico than Spain. When people ask me what extraction I am, I don't say 'Spanish,' but 'Mexican.'"

Jeannine was torn between commenting and savoring the superb *huevos rancheros,* but her curiosity won over her taste buds. "Is that technically accurate, though? When people ask such a thing, they usually mean your bloodstrain, don't they?"

Miguel was deftly buttering a tortilla, rolling it into a white panatela. "That was in the old days," he answered. "It used to be assumed that your bloodline was the same as your nationality. Tell me," he said, leaning forward, a very earnest expression on his face, "when you tell people you're an American, do you expect them to believe that you're an Indian?"

"Why, no, of course not," she said, smiling at what she considered a preposterous supposition.

"But, my dear Miss Wellman, by your own logic, an American is, after all, an Indian. Everyone else claims this nation as an adopted country. The only true American is the Indian, the rest of you are immigrants."

Jeannine stared at him for a moment, then realized that he was right. She smiled at him shyly. "I hadn't really thought it through, I suppose," she said, pushing a wisp of her hair out of her eyes, and moving the salt cellar to the corner of the table where the playful breeze agitated the corner of the tablecloth.

"The same is true of Mexico, or the rest of South America. It may have belonged to the Indians originally, but the Spanish have been there for so long that they are no longer truly Spanish in their attitudes, in their allegiance. There has been quite a bit of integration, of course, over the centuries . . . a few holdouts, if you care about such things as blind pride in a pure bloodline. But we have Irish Mexicans, Swedish Mexicans, German Mexicans . . . and Spanish Mexicans. But tell the average American that you're a Mexican, and he immediately sees a peon holding a sombrero."

Jeannine laughed at his imagery. "We're not all that bad," she said, "that naive."

"Ah, perhaps not all — but most. It's very discouraging, Miss Wellman, to have to spend your life explaining to your fellow Americans that not all Mexicans are Indians."

"Then why do you bother?" she'd said before she could stop herself. It was not a very tactful question and she was sorry the

46

moment the words had tumbled out.

Miguel stared at her intently for only a second, then his eyes became guarded and he permitted himself a slight smile. "Perhaps because there is a little bit of Don Quixote in all of us. This widespread American misconception has become my windmill."

"And does the señora think of herself as Mexican also?" Jeannine asked, pouring them both more coffee.

"My grandmother is an old woman, Miss Wellman. In fact, she is not truly my grandmother but my great-grandmother . . . none of us knows exactly how old she really is. That was your next question, wasn't it?"

She flushed at his perception, and nodded. "Then what you're saying is that at her age, she would be more likely to identify with Spain than with Mexico?"

"In many ways, yes. But, you see, Ignacio de Lorca was her second husband, not her first. And Ignacio de Lorca was a Mexican–Spanish blood, yes, but Mexican allegiance. And it was his family that . . . well, it's a very long story. I'm sure that Grandmother will tell you herself when she's feeling better. She loves to talk about the old days."

A silence fell between them, neither awkward nor peaceful, until Miguel lit up a corona and exhaled the gray, pungent smoke.

47

"I've a rather unpleasant question I must ask you, Miss Wellman."

Her gaze broke from the vista before them and turned directly into Miguel's; she couldn't know what was in his mind, but the tone of his voice, the level inquisition of his eyes, made her uncomfortable, even somewhat apprehensive.

"Your silence suggests your consent," he said after a moment. "Tell me, why are you here? Why would a woman of your obvious qualifications want to bury herself in such an uninteresting job, so isolated from the rest of the world. Though I cannot tell you my reasons for needing to know that, at least not for a while, may I assure you that I am not merely prying."

"I see," Jeannine said, shaking her head as he offered to pour her more coffee. "There's no dark secret about it, Mr. de Lorca," she began, his last name awkward on her lips since she usually thought of him as Miguel. "I'm in rather poor health. My doctor advised me to get out of the city, to get away from any high-pressured work, and to live a less panicked life. The position your grandmother offered seemed ideal. That's all there is to it."

"Poor health," he repeated, flicking his cigar ashes into the ceramic ashtray at his elbow. "Nothing serious, I hope."

It was Jeannine's turn to smile. How like a man, she thought, to cringe from any form of illness. "Rheumatic fever. I've had it for years. Recurrent, I'm afraid. Pressure and worry are very bad for me. Very bad," she said again, but noticing his expression, she let her voice trail off.

"Tension," he said, nearly in an accusatory voice, "tension or hostile relations . . . these things could bring on another attack?"

"Yes."

"I'm a lawyer, Miss Wellman, not a doctor. Please forgive my ignorance. What is the worst that could happen to you in the event of another attack?"

Jeannine had lived with her illness for so long that she no longer conveyed any strong emotion when discussing it. "The worst, Mr. de Lorca, would be a massive stroke . . . and my death."

For a fraction of time, she thought she could detect his mixed reaction to her words; she thought she had seen compassion, perhaps even a little pity, a moment's protectiveness. But it was gone from his eyes before she could be certain. It could just as easily have been a mirroring of a rapid mind swiftly tallying the knowledge for its own purposes. And Jeannine was convinced that even if she lived to be three hundred years old, she would never forget his next words, or their deadly, cold delivery just before he stood and left her all alone on that lovely balcony above the Pacific.

"I hope you have not come to the wrong place, Miss Wellman. For your sake, I hope not."

Chapter 4

The bright cheerfulness of the morning began to dissipate about eleven o' clock, and
Jeannine was compelled to fetch a sweater
against the chill damp wind from the sea.
She returned to the den where she had been
typing answers to an amazing number of letters from people requesting endorsements
from the señora for this proposition, or that
legislative bill, or invitations to luncheons
and teas. The letters were usually fawning,
and prefaced with "While I know you normally do not accept social invitations, I am
certain that our particular cause will appeal
. . ." and so on. Everyone, it seemed,
wanted something from la señora. Jeannine
had only been working for her about a
week, but she could have told them that la
señora was not likely to endorse, sponsor,
or encourage any community project she
herself had not originated. Even while bed-
ridden, still recuperating from the mild sei-
zure the night of Jeannine's arrival, la señora
summoned and dictated and ran her household with willful determination.

There was something foreboding about this day, Jeannine decided; the breakfast with Miguel de Lorca, and the sudden shift in the weather. It was as if some sadistic fate had smugly lifted the veil of the future for Jeannine, showing her how charming life might be and then dropped the veil back down with the force of an iron door shutting on such possibilities.

Jeannine stood up and walked over to the French windows at the far side of the den, staring out to sea and trying to dispel the heavy mood that was enveloping her. Jeannine was not especially given to "moods," and she could only assume that she was still too new at "Puerta de Paz" to feel completely at ease. As she gazed at the frothing surf assaulting the reefs so far below the hacienda, she wondered just how long it would take her to "settle in."

The unexpected sharp ring of the telephone startled Jeannine out of her introspective daydream, and she jumped at the harsh intrusion. As she turned toward the desk, she saw la señora poised in the doorway to the den.

"I suggest, child, that you answer the phone," Mrs. de Lorca said, a slight smile on her lips.

Again Jeannine experienced a sense of

hopeless incompetence, inexplicable and upsetting. She lifted the receiver. "Puerta de Paz," she said, and glanced at la señora as the caller introduced himself. "Just a moment, please," she said, covering the mouthpiece. "John de Lorca?" she announced to the woman who now stood at the windows precisely where Jeannine had been a moment before.

La señora, standing like an apparition before the gray troubled sky, nodded slowly, waving her hand with graceful impatience as if to say Jeannine should have known. "My *other* grandson, Miguel's cousin. What does he want?"

Jeannine thought she detected an approving fondness for this man in the old woman's voice. "He just heard that you'd not been well . . . he's inquiring. . . ."

"*Coraje!* 'He's inquiring!' He wants to find out how close to death I am! My will is the best-kept secret since the hidden wealth of Mussolini! Here, give me that fool instrument!" She carefully crossed to the ebony desk and took the receiver from Jeannine. "*Oye, Juanillo,* I know why you've called, you transparent rascal! What? *Andale, mijo,* I am an old woman and not to be played with. Your little jokes fall upon stone ears."

Jeannine made every effort to not listen to the conversation, but it was difficult to ignore. The warmth in the woman's deep voice, the totally unexpected coquetry, made indifference virtually impossible. John, apparently, made his grandmother — or great-grandmother — laugh; Miguel, on the other hand, seemed to evoke only her stern expectations from him. Twice, when Jeannine had passed by la señora's bedroom, she had heard Miguel's basso in deep exchange with la señora behind closed doors. While Jeannine had been unable to distinguish any words, the tone had been unmistakable: argumentative, disapproving, and very demanding. Whatever it was that the old woman and Miguel discussed, it was obviously of enormous importance to them both. Evidently, la señora looked upon John as her favorite, an utterly useless young man — from her tone — but an endearing one. Jeannine wondered about John, trying to form an image of a carefree, dashing fellow; but the stern countenance of Miguel superimposed itself and she had to abandon the attempt.

Hearing la señora laugh for the very first time brought Jeannine back to the present. It was a strange laugh, hearty yet delivered slowly, as if only so much mirth could be permitted without harm, and Jeannine could not resist glancing in the woman's direction. She sat at her mammoth desk, frail, overshadowed by its masculine design, with her fragile hand at her throat. Her delicate frame moved almost imperceptibly, but her eyes shone with loving amusement.

"*Bueno,* Juanillo, but do not expect too much from me. I am yet very exhausted, not quite back to normal," she said, then her expression clouded slightly. "What? Olga too? *Ay, qué lata!* Yes, yes, I know what she thinks of me — perhaps better than you do. *Está bien.* I'll tell Chata and Manuel to prepare things. *Adiós.*"

The woman replaced the receiver and turned to glance at Jeannine with an expression that clearly showed both humor and annoyance. "It would seem that you are about to meet some of the family, Jeannine. Juanillo is driving down from San Francisco with his sister. We shall have house guests for a while."

She paused, and Jeannine could see the woman determining all the necessary arrangements in her mind, swiftly, decisively. To watch the old woman's eyes vitally alternating from black to dark brown, back to black as each thought was invoked, cubbyholed, and filed in place was intriguing. In la señora's mind, the guests had arrived, been entertained, and she was already back to her normal routine. It was impossible for anyone not to be somewhat awed in her presence; the woman was formidable and fascinating.

Jeannine, for the first time since her arrival at "Puerta de Paz," felt totally at ease and filled with conviviality. They were all seated at the elaborately carved oak dining table, and a superb Beaune was generously ever-present in their crystal goblets. Olga de Lorca sat alone opposite Jeannine, who was seated next to John. Miguel and la señora faced each other at opposite ends of the table. Jeannine was delighted to have a woman near her own age to talk to, especially since Olga proved to be a natural conversationalist; the girl could rattle on ceaselessly on the most disparate topics, yet always with great mirth and animation, so that disinterest or boredom was impossible.

John couldn't have been more dissimilar from Miguel if they had clasped hands as children and sworn toward that end. While not a babbler, as was Olga, John was charming, attentive, and openly admiring of Jeannine. "More béarnaise, Jeannie?" he asked solicitously, bestowing upon her a nickname she'd not heard since childhood.

She smiled but refused, glancing from la señora's warmly endearing gaze that rested upon John to Miguel's sullen scowl as he intently ravaged his chateaubriand.

"I adore your kaftan, Jeannine," Olga said. "Wherever did you find it?"

"Down in the village, just yesterday, as a matter of fact. It was marked down . . ." she began to say, and then realized that such things would be of no importance to anyone raised with an endless supply of money.

"How I adore bargains! You must give me the name of the shop later, or perhaps we could go there tomorrow? If only Doña Josefina were not quite so cautious with the family fortune . . . perhaps bargains would not be quite the thrill they seem lately." Olga cast a pouting, teasing glance toward the family matriarch.

La señora nodded with elaborate dignity toward Olga. "If I were not so careful, there would be no family fortune to guard."

"Especially with your tastes," John chided his sister.

"Mine! You've got to be joking! I'm not the darling of the polo pony set!"

Miguel raised his dark head and momentarily stared across at his grandmother, then in a nearly emotionless tone said, "If the two of you must behave like children, perhaps I should send you to bed without dessert."

"Now look here, Mike, that's no way . . ." John said, flushing deeply and not daring to look away from the silver candlestick only inches from his plate.

"The name is not 'Mike,' nor is yours John. If it pleases you to live the life of a gringo playboy, that's your business . . . but I'd appreciate it if you didn't automatically include me."

"Well, it's a lot better than your tradition-bound extremism," Olga threw back. "You *do* carry the aura of the conquistador a bit far for life in the '70s."

Miguel stiffened, but said nothing. What seemed even worse, no one said anything for a full, heavy minute or two. But Olga, slave to her tongue, finally broke the awkwardness of the moment. "Have you been to the mission yet?" she asked Jeannine, as if they'd just been discussing sightseeing.

Jeannine smiled, almost more from relief than interest. "Yes. It was fascinating. I'd never been to a mission before."

"What do you suppose Junípero Serra would think if he could see the old place now?" John said swiftly, taking up the opportunity to regain their earlier lightheart-edness.

Jeannine glanced at him, at the tanned features so unlike Miguel's, at the way his dark-brown hair glistened with red high-lights from so much time spent in the sun. He seemed ingenuous compared to Miguel, and she surprised herself in the realization: Why should she compare the two men? But la señora's reply precluded further specula-tion.

"Why not ask what Alexander of Mace-don would think of Athens? Or more to the point, what the Costanoans would think?"

"I thought the local Indians were called Rumsens," Olga said, plopping a small po-tato into her mouth.

La señora smiled tolerantly. "Olga, his-tory was never your forte, I fear. The Rum-sens were a subgroup of the Costanoans."

"Where are the native Indians now?" Jeannine inquired, genuinely interested. She had not noticed anyone in the area who could possibly fit the stereotype of "Indian."

"They were never a very large group, Jeannine," Miguel answered. "Estimates vary, but certainly there were never more than about ten thousand Costanoans here."

Jeannine was flattered by Miguel's reply. It was the first time that evening that he

59

had purposely spoken to her only, and she couldn't help but wonder if he were not penitent about his earlier conduct with his cousins. Encouraged by his attention, she persisted. "But what happened to them?"

He looked directly into her eyes, then, with the candlelight reflecting in his somber eyes, a slow, patient smile flickered on his lips. "You really are interested, aren't you?" he said; and pleased with her question, he continued. "The Indians died out gradually. The white man was very democratic in his gifts to all tribes in this country: diphtheria, cholera, syphillis . . . by 1834, about one seventh of them still survived."

"Don't get him started," John laughed, "or we'll never get away from the table. He's as bad as Doña Josefina on the subject."

"Juanillo, don't be impudent!" la señora chided mildly. "Actually, my dear, many of them also intermarried with the Spanish settlers. It was encouraged, you know, unlike other nationalities which felt that intermarriage was demeaning." She raised her glass, closing her eyes briefly, then said, "To the nearly extinct Costanoans . . . may their island where the sun sets be safe so that they may be born again in peace and harmony."

No one at the table left the toast unmet.

Jeannine was discreet enough not to pursue the subject any further. The balance of the supper was accompanied by Olga's effervescent conversation, punctuated by John's good-natured repartee, and la señora's indulgence. And, while Miguel said little thereafter, Jeannine was constantly aware of his scrutiny, as if he were evaluating her, contrasting her to his cousins and his own rigid and unspoken principles. She couldn't shake the feeling that Miguel could read her mind; could see straight through her as easily as holding gauze to sunlight. And, surprisingly, she was rather pleased about it. True, it made her somewhat uncomfortable, but not as much as it had during breakfast that morning . . . and at least he was not ignoring her. She knew that she was placing undue importance upon his attention to her; yet, when she felt his attention veering away, she experienced a sense of loss disproportionate to what little relationship they'd thus far established.

There was no doubt in her mind, sipping coffee, listening to Olga and John entertain their grandmother, that Miguel had some kind of hold on her psyche. If only he weren't such a sour person, if only Miguel had some of the charm of his cousin John, if only . . .

"Penny," John's voice broke into her thoughts.

"Oh, I *am* sorry," Jeannine said, hoping no one would notice her embarrassment.

"C'mon," he said softly, "let's go for a ride into town. We'll throw off our shoes and walk barefooted in the surf."

"Ay, Juanillo," Doña Josefina said with exasperation, *"no vayas a pescar un resfriado!"*

He had already risen and was standing by the woman's chair, and smiling, he bent over and kissed the top of her head. "Don't worry, my precious worrywart, we're white men and able to withstand the white man's common cold."

John took Jeannine's small hand and nearly lifted her from the velvet-cushioned chair. "Let's go see what the other half is up to tonight!"

They had already driven halfway down the mountainside before Jeannine realized she'd failed to say good night to anyone — not even to Miguel.

Chapter 5

Jeannine, resting her head against the car seat, still carried with her the music of the evening. John had taken her to Esperanto's, the local hippie bistro in Carmel — except, as Jeannine had commented to him earlier, it was like no other "hippie" place she'd ever visited before. In most of their hangouts, there was an air of rebellion, of surliness, that was not present at the Esperanto. Here the young and middle-aged mingled good-naturedly, not caring if anyone was Establishment or anti-Establishment — the only qualification for a wonderful evening was an open heart. Anyone who wished to could join in the singing, or pick up a guitar and entertain; it was more like a family get-together comprised of congenial strangers.

It had been a lovely evening, one to be remembered and savored. They had sipped wine, and she had been mildly surprised to find that John had a singularly good singing voice for folk music, and that he played the guitar with more feeling than virtuosity. His rendition of *Barbara Allen* had a lovely, haunting quality, as if he had known her well; and it endeared him to her. She began to look at John in an entirely new way . . . not as the super-charming jetsetter, but as a sensible, feeling man. She was seeing an entirely different side to this cousin of Miguel, and she very much approved of what she saw.

"Have a nice time?" John's voice broke into her thoughts.

She glanced at his calm face, and observed the way he drove the car with masculine assurance. "Yes," she replied softly. "A very nice time . . . thank you." She was tempted to take his hand and hold it, to show him with some gentle, physical gesture how much she had appreciated the evening, and his company. But she feared he might misinterpret the gesture, might think her bold or brazen or god-knows-what, and she decided against it. She didn't want to do anything that could possibly break their mood or dispel that moment's closeness.

He glanced over at her briefly, smiling at her, and she could only dimly make out his features in the inky shadows. The dashboard illuminated his face, casting an eerie glow, which — had she not already felt so warmly attracted to John — might have frightened her with the gargoyle-like trans-

64

formation the greenish cast produced.

In moments they were wending their way up the sharp curves of the mountainside, driving a little faster than she would have preferred, but she realized that John knew the road well. "The old road," as Manuel had called it, with its sharp curves and sheer drops camouflaged by foliage and the lovely California lilacs Jeannine had initially thought to be heather. She felt so totally secure in John's hands that she uncharacteristically didn't sit up to mentally do the driving.

But when they rounded the curve where the majestic fir known as "el viejo" signaled their proximity to the house, Jeannine began to feel that something was wrong. No sooner did she sense this, than John started instructing her in gentle but urgent tones.

"I expect you to do as I say, Jeannie, and without any questions. Get down on the floorboard, curl up, and cover your face with your arms. . . ."

"But . . ." Jeannine began to ask.

"Don't argue! Do what I say, and do it *now!* There's something very wrong with the steering . . . I'm losing control of the car. Quickly, Jeannie, quickly!"

His tone was not panicked in the least, but it would not tolerate any contradiction.

Almost mechanically she crouched to the floor of the car, concerned but not truly fearful. Had John said that one of the tires had a slow leak, she could have had a very similar reaction.

"Relax yourself completely," he commanded. "This is going to be tricky. . . ."

Almost instantly, Jeannine felt as if the car were flying, felt the front wheels leave the road and the violent lurching as it careened over boulders and shrubs, and then a sense of soaring smoothness. The silence of the night was complemented by the engine's purr, as if the automobile were a part of it, and suddenly Jeannine felt very light-headed, felt her blood begin to pound at her temples — and knew fear as she had never known it before.

"My God!" John screamed.

And Jeannine was only dimly aware of the car's impact as it returned to earth.

First the voices — strange, distorted voices — drifted through to her. They seemed anxious, even perhaps somewhat displeased, as if she'd done something very naughty and her punishment was under discussion. Her head was throbbing wildly, and the familiar tightness about her heart sat like some behemoth blocking her breath.

The voices undulated through her mind like electrical impulses; she could feel the sounds as if she were being given frequent low-voltage stimuli, and it occurred to her that she might very well be dead, that this was her limbo, her waiting room with Fate. Or perhaps, her quasi-delirious mind conjectured, just perhaps she was privy to the discourses of her reincarnation . . . her soul was being reassigned at that very moment, without her knowledge, consent, or approval. The mere thought of such a decision without her consent began to anger her.

She blacked out again and knew nothing.

When she regained consciousness, it was totally. Jeannine's eyes opened slowly; the sunlight in her bedroom was muted by closed shutters. This time she was fully aware, completely awake, as if she had been in hibernation and the stirrings of spring had sparked a primitive, instinctual awakening. She tried to turn her head and felt only a dull pain with the effort, but was both surprised and very touched to see la señora seated at the writing desk, her arthritic hands laboriously penning something in the dim light of the bedroom. Jeannine had no idea of how long she had lain in bed, of how many hours or days had passed; and she only dimly recalled the terrifying last seconds before the car had gone off the road.

With a shock of cognizance, she tried to ask la señora what had happened to John, if he was all right . . . but the only sound that escaped her bruised lips was "John? . . ."

La señora lifted her head slowly, as if unsure that she had heard any sound, then turned and gazed at Jeannine's recumbent form. Her large, penetrating eyes were fixed upon Jeannine, assessing the degree of her awareness. "How do you feel, *niña?*" she asked in a deep-throated whisper.

Jeannine tried to smile, but she couldn't quite manage it. She watched la señora rise from the chair and cross the room gracefully until she was standing at the side of her Sheraton four-poster, her face a mask of equanimity. "You have given me some very tedious moments, Jeannine. I did not retain your services in order to watch you rest. . . ."

Had Jeannine not already learned to cope and understand la señora's cantankerous and stiff exterior, she might have reacted either with justifiable anger, or cringed with guilt. As it was, her soul smiled with absolute understanding of what lay beneath the woman's words. Doggedly refusing to admit how very worried she had been, Doña Josefina chose to chastise. Jeannine was certain that the woman would far prefer to spank her out of sheer relief and anger at having been put through such concern and anguish. Jeannine tried to extend her hand to the woman, to show her that she was truly sorry to have put her through any suffering at all, but la señora anticipated the gesture, and covered her hand with her own tiny dry palm, squeezing gently, reassuringly.

"*Basta!* You are now getting well, and that is all that counts. You are to rest, *niña*, to regain your strength — you were very lucky that you were not killed."

"And John?" Jeannine managed to say.

La señora nodded stiffly, as if confirming that since only children and fools walk in God's good graces, John had survived the accident. "A broken arm, nothing more," she said.

Jeannine was immensely relieved. "It . . . it was n-not his fault," she managed to say, exhaustion already beginning to claim her.

"Perhaps, *niña*, perhaps. Do not think of that now. Rest. The doctor will be here shortly, and I shall wake you then. Perhaps in a half hour or so, with some weak tea and some strong brandy. You must sleep now . . . shh . . . close your eyes . . . yes

. . . that is better . . . just sleep. . . ."

Dr. Ortíz listened to her heart with all the bedside manner of a tax collector. He was so formal in his manner that all he really required to complete the image was a morning suit and top hat. When he straightened up, he removed his stethoscope and stood clicking the ends together distractedly. "The shock has done more damage than the bruises," he announced. "But then," he said, shooting a glance over to la señora, "not every young lady has three physicians in attendance."

Jeannine could not miss the iciness in his tone. "Three?" she asked.

La señora shook her head at the doctor, *tsk*ing at him, then explained. "Such professional insecurity does not become you, Dr. Ortíz. Especially since you were in Sacramento at the convention. Did you expect me to just let those two remain in the wreckage, awaiting your return?"

"But to call in Aaron Franklin!" Dr. Ortíz protested mildly.

"He *is* a doctor. There was no one else available at that hour! And, you forget, at one time he was a very close friend of the family."

Dr. Ortíz shook his head, clearly unable

to reconcile himself to the intrusion of this other doctor. "Well, at least he didn't do any actual harm." Dr. Ortíz's voice trailed off feebly.

"You said three doctors," Jeannine interjected.

"I took the liberty of phoning your Dr. Sternig," la señora explained. "I knew only that you had been in poor health, under some sort of strain, and I thought it wisest to consult with your regular physician under the circumstances — you could have had some fatal allergy to the medication, perhaps, and I did not wish to take any unnecessary chances."

Dr. Ortíz cleared his throat, sensing the accusation beneath la señora's remarks. "Well, all of that is by the board now. No harm done."

"Thanks to Dr. Franklin," the woman shot back at him. "If he had not immediately recognized your heart condition, well, we have much to thank him for."

Jeannine glanced from the doctor to la señora, torn between appreciating the nature of their bickering, and just wishing they'd both stop it and leave her in peace. Despite the undercurrent of their exchange, Jeannine knew full well the respect that existed between them; and she resolved to call upon this mysterious Dr. Aaron Franklin as soon as she was ambulatory. It could not be very flattering to be called in only for an emergency, and then dismissed like a dull child. And too, she would have to write a long explanatory letter to Vincent Sternig and reassure him that she was quite all right. It had been an accident — nothing more. Accidents happen to everyone. She only hoped that John was not taking the entire matter too much to heart, not feeling overly at fault or guilty.

As if on cue, there was a light rapping at the bedroom door, and seconds later John entered. He was limping only slightly — the result of his knee having hit the steering post — and his left arm was in a cast. Nonetheless, he was wearing flares and a tennis sweater and looked very much as if he'd just stopped by on his way to the courts. Ignoring both the doctor and his grandmother, he crossed over to Jeannine's side, and planted a very chaste kiss on her forehead. Still leaning over her, he whispered, "If anything had happened to you, I don't think I could have survived."

His words, his facial expression, the very attitude of his body conveyed sincerity, and deep affection — perhaps even more than affection. Jeannine fought to hold back her tears, to keep her poise. Her entire being was responding to his tender concern. Perhaps it was the emotional release of the accident, or her still weakened condition, but Jeannine began to cry — silently, with huge tears rolling down her cheeks. No man had ever shown her such solicitude. She was accustomed to the Hollywood male, the super-sophisticate and the pseudo-sophisticate, all with only one purpose in mind. John's attitude was something totally new to her; unexpected, sweet, and securely exciting. When he looked into her eyes, his, too, were clouded with tears, and she knew that they were both sharing a moment neither of them would ever forget. They had faced the prospect of violent death together, and they had both survived. It was not the sort of experience anyone could take lightly, and they both knew it had created a strong bond between them.

Even as these thoughts were running through her head, she could hear the doctor and la señora discussing her health and care, and then la señora insisting that John leave the room so that Jeannine could rest. Jeannine knew that something was happening between herself and John . . . something beautiful. It was such a new, wonderful sensation, that she wished someone would open the shutters, would let in the sunlight and the crisp fresh salt air.

She did not hear the doctor or John leave her room, nor did she hear la señora return to the writing desk. Her eyes closed, and a soft breeze had stolen through the shutters to caress her to sleep. . . .

Chapter 6

"And I tell you that it happened all of a sudden, without warning! How the hell could it have been *my* fault!" John yelled at Miguel, who was standing near the walk-in fireplace in the living room. John was seated, holding a highball, one arm thrown over the back of the divan and his legs propped up on the coffee table before him.

It was not the first time Jeannine had overheard the two men arguing about what caused the auto accident only a week before. She was practically back to her usual self, with her few bruises swiftly fading, and the last thing in the world Jeannine wanted to discuss or contemplate was that awful night. While she realized that the insurance company would want to know all about the cause in order to pin responsibility, she could not understand why it was Miguel harangued at John about it. It was done and over, it was past — what business was it of Miguel's? But she was relatively certain she could answer her own question; Miguel had not failed to notice what was going on between John and herself. With no small amount of smug satisfaction, Jeannine had observed Miguel's frown, lips pursed with silent annoyance, whenever John made some reference to his feelings for Jeannine, or when a glance passed between them that clearly indicated their growing affection.

She realized she was probably reacting like a child, going through some "So there!" foolishness, but she couldn't help it. She had tried to win Miguel over, to earn his respect; she recognized that it was probably asking too much to hope for his friendship. Perhaps if Olga and John had not come to stay after the morning she and Miguel had had breakfast together on the terrace . . . perhaps if they'd had a little more time to get to know each other . . . But they hadn't. Any opportunity they might have had to truly get to know each other had been interrupted with John's arrival — and the accident. Which was yet another reason for Jeannine's attitude toward Miguel: As far as she knew, not once had he inquired about her well-being or stopped in to see how she was coming along. She could not forgive his rudeness; one would be more considerate of an animal than Miguel had been of her. With the exception of needling John about the accident itself, Miguel had shown absolutely no concern about her health.

Jeannine was genuinely attracted to John, to his casual good-humor and his attentiveness, but she also derived a perverse pleasure from Miguel's disapproval. If he were not so pigheaded, so consumed with his role as sentinel of the manor, he would be included in their conversations and activities.

Despite the incredible scenic beauty of the valley and the coastline of Carmel-by-the-Sea, despite the magnificent charm and warmth of "Puerta de Paz," there was something very wrong here, which Jeannine could not quite pinpoint. Several times during her convalescence, she had dimly perceived voices in argument — but never clearly enough even to establish the speaker, much less distinguish words. She knew that Miguel and la señora had exchanged unpleasantries from time to time, but since John's arrival the arguments seemed to have increased. She did not know if they were between John and Miguel, Miguel and his grandmother, or perhaps all three of them.

Olga had returned to San Francisco the morning after the accident. It was just as well, Jeannine thought; as much as she had enjoyed meeting her, she was in no mood to exchange idle banter. Moreover, Olga seemed to bring out the worst in Miguel —

if such a scowling soul could darken any more. Yet Jeannine fully accepted that whatever it was that hung so heavily over "Puerta de Paz," it was none of her business. If la señora wanted her to know what was going on, la señora would have revealed it to her. A family squabble, no doubt . . . there was nothing she could do about it, and she certainly would never dare inquire . . . so she attempted to put it out of her mind.

The way Miguel continued to cross-examine John about the accident, however, infuriated her. He didn't have to speak to John in that imperious tone of voice, as if John were some recalcitrant child in the presence of Olympian superiority. John had given her a very simple explanation; she had not found any reason to doubt his account of it — why did Miguel? As John had explained, the car had been handling perfectly well the entire evening. Then, suddenly and without any warning, he'd realized that the steering wheel was not responding too well, that it seemed to have a point where it shuddered a little . . . and he'd made a mental note to take it in to the mechanic the next day. And now again, as she paused momentarily in the foyer to don her brightly-colored scarf, Miguel was forcing

John to rake through the accounting.

"Surely it occurred to you that something serious could be wrong," Miguel hammered.

John ran his fingers through his hair in a gesture of complete exasperation. "For God's sake, Miguel, we weren't even a quarter of a mile from home! Why would I do anything but keep going?"

"What if you'd had a blowout? Would you just have kept right on going? An old horse returning to the stable? What kind of a fool are you!"

"Now, see here!"

"All right, all right. I'm sorry I said that. But you damned nearly got killed, and naturally I'm very upset about that entire incident."

John stood and went to the sideboard to pour himself a fresh drink. "So did Jeannie, if you'll recall."

Miguel nodded almost to himself. "Yes. So did Jeannine. I've not forgotten."

"And give me credit for having the brains to get her down on the floorboard," John said, straightening his shoulders defiantly.

Miguel snorted like some indignant bull. "You were damned lucky she didn't get crushed by the engine. That was not the wisest thing for you to do. . . ."

Jeannine could hear the tightness in Miguel's voice returning and knew they were in for another round of debate. She had already said everything she had to say about that evening, there was nothing she could do to break it up or give any additional light. With a sigh of tolerance, she opened the front door and stepped out into the brisk morning air, letting the door close on the unpleasantness behind her. She took a deep breath, her lungs momentarily hurting from the invigorating, penetrating clean air, and paused a moment to scan the vista before her. Masses of manzanita grew among the pines and on out to the coastline, where, from the distance, the water seemed deceptively calm. Jeannine never tired of the view — and though she knew the feeling was ridiculous, nonetheless, standing before the house and gazing out at such magnificence gave her a sense of godliness, of omnipotence.

Jeannine, who had driven down to the village to pick up a few stationery items for la señora, decided it was such an absolutely lovely day that she had to stop. She could not resist parking the small VW on Scenic Street and heading for the beach, which was nearly deserted. Removing her sandals, she began to walk north in the icy water which danced about her bare feet. When she reached the dunes, she sat down on the cool sand and hugged her knees to her, staring out at the incredibly blue ocean, with its windswept whitecaps like miniature armies mobilizing for a beachhead.

The morning sun seemed particularly warm whenever the wind subsided, and squeaking gulls soared in sweeping circles against a backdrop of heavy cumulus clouds. She was so lost in reverie, so physically attuned to her environs, that she was oblivious to intrusions. And then, still nearly trancelike, she was dimly aware of a man's voice saying her name. She forced herself to bring her mind back to the present.

What she focussed upon was a man about seventy years old, with an extraordinarily kindly face and snowy white hair. His eyes were dark brown, with laugh wrinkles surrounding them. There were furrows in his tanned brow and it was easy to discern that here was a man who had spent a very great deal of time in the sun and the wind.

"How nice to see your swift recovery, Miss Wellman," his resonant voice enthused.

"I'm afraid . . ." Jeannine said hesitantly, trying to smile her way out of the embarrassment of the situation.

"Oh, I am sorry," he laughed. "Of course you wouldn't know who I am. I'm Aaron Franklin."

"Of course," Jeannine responded with a self-deprecating shrug, "the doctor Mrs. de Lorca phoned after the accident."

He eased himself down to the dune cautiously, then pulled out a pipe and began to tamp tobacco into it. "Mind if I join you for a bit? It's quite a walk from my place to here."

She nodded her welcome of his company. There was something very reassuring about the man; fatherly, perhaps, but more than that. Any doctor who does not introduce himself as a doctor, she thought, must be quite a man!

"How're you getting on at 'Puerta de Paz,' Miss Wellman? Finding it a trifle remote or lonely?"

He asked the question in the same tone of voice he might have asked a long-time patient how his lumbago was doing; cordial, genuinely interested, and with a touch of humor about the limitations of medicine. She closed her hazel eyes for an instant, weighing his question seriously, then replied, "No. Not really. I'm either too busy . . ."

"Or incapacitated," he volunteered.

". . . or too in love with the beauty of this area to miss people."

She watched him light his pipe, and enjoyed the pungent-sweet smell of his tobacco mixed with the salt air. He puffed thoughtfully, squinting out to sea. "Understand young John is staying on for a while."

"Yes," she answered, not knowing what else to say.

"Nice lad. Trifle wild, but a good lad."

"Wild?"

"Oh, not really wild, I guess. Just something more of a playboy than I'd like if he were my own son. That sort of thing. I'll never fully understand a man who does not work at something."

Jeannine laughed lightly. "Well, he does. He works at not working!" As soon as the words came out she wished she had not said them. She didn't really know this man, after all, and a remark like that could easily be misinterpreted.

"Yes," Aaron Franklin said, laughing, "he's very successful at that. And Miguel?"

Jeannine thought she detected a change in his tone of voice, but couldn't be sure. "Oh, the same as usual, I suppose." Surely *that* was vague enough! Although Mrs. de Lorca had staunchly defended Dr. Franklin,

Jeannine did not know what position this man held in their family affairs. Was the doctor fishing for information? Or merely politely inquiring?

Aaron Franklin immediately covered her hand with his and wrapped her thin fingers beneath his warm, stubby ones. "You don't have to protect them from me," he said with a disarming smile. "I've known the boys all their lives . . . and I've known Josefina almost my own entire life." He withdrew his hand, and they were silent for a few moments; both wrapped in their own thoughts. "I had hoped, when I heard that you were coming out here to live, that Miguel might learn to laugh a little, might come out of his shell. Surely, with a charming redhead on the premises, he cannot continue to haunt the halls with his disapproval."

His words carried such warmth in them, such compassion, that Jeannine instantly felt herself in the company of an ally. As if a floodgate had been thrown open, she was filled with questions about the de Lorca family, her tongue tripping with impatience to voice her curiosity. "Was Miguel always so terribly serious?" she asked. "Even as a child?"

The doctor drew on his pipe, giving the question heavy consideration before replying. "Yes. Yes, I think he was. He was never a frivolous child, or I suppose it would be more accurate to say he simply was never a child. Miguel was born an old man . . . at heart, anyway. I suppose if you believe in reincarnation, you might say he's a very old soul."

There didn't seem to be anything she could say to that. She wished she'd known Miguel as a boy, been able to grow up with him so she would fully understand him; she could have comforted him when he was filled with doubts, or shown him how to laugh so that life would not pain him so. But Miguel could not permit such closeness at this point in his life; the wall of invisible isolation had been built, brick by brick, with a determination molded by the outside world, a world he hadn't learned to laugh at. In her mind, as she wistfully stared out to sea, she saw a sturdy little boy, with strong, rounded legs in short pants, and a crop of unruly black hair framing a poignantly serious face, a face that could only frown at the world. And she wished she could hold that child, hold him close and offer him love and reassurances . . . but, of course, that was impossible.

Chapter 7

Manuel was serving cocktails by the time Jeannine returned to the house, shortly after twelve. Lunch would be ready soon, she knew, and la señora was enjoying her customary noontime cocktail — "to improve my appetite," as she frequently explained, her austere expression betrayed by a dancing twinkle in her eyes.

John and Miguel were also present, and the tension between them was obvious, while la señora seemed pensive and somewhat remote. Sensing the atmosphere, Jeannine entered the room quietly and chose a chair closer to Doña Josefina than to either of the men. Manuel smiled rather nervously as he poured Jeannine's drink and brought it to her, his thin, wizened face masklike in his obvious attempt to keep his own counsel.

It was la señora who finally broke the silence in the room. She took a dainty sip from her glass, and then gazing at Jeannine, said in nearly a monotone, "Miguel has some rather unpleasant information, child.

Something you are entitled to know about."

Jeannine's heart began to pound in her breast, and her palms became moist. She knew that whatever it was Miguel had to say, it was going to be more than merely "unpleasant." She still was not sufficiently recovered from the effects of the accident, the strain on her heart and her nerves, to be in complete control of herself, and she wished she could run to her room for her pills before listening to whatever news Miguel was to convey — but she didn't quite dare leave them in what was, obviously, a crucial moment of tension.

"Bueno, Miguel, dile," Doña Josefina urged.

Miguel didn't look at Jeannine as he began, but crossed to the French doors and stood with his back to her. "I received the mechanic's report on the car," he said, adding in a soft voice, "about an hour ago." His pause seemed interminable. Miguel turned around, then, facing Jeannine with an expression in his eyes that seemed to say "Hold on to yourself, don't let it upset you too much."

"Go on, go on!" la señora prodded.

Miguel shrugged. "The car had been tampered with, Jeannine. The king pins had been nearly sawn through and then re-

87

placed. The accident was . . . was not an accident," he said with a trailing voice.

Jeannine could do nothing more than stare from John's face to Miguel's to la señora's. Not an accident? "But . . . why? . . . or who? . . ." she asked falteringly.

"Some kid, I'm sure," John offered. "Maybe resenting my expensive car while we were at Esperanto's."

"Wouldn't that be an excessive amount of trouble?" la señora asked John. "Why not just slash the tires or some other, easier way of showing resentment?"

"So it was a very enterprising kid . . . maybe his father owns a garage," John said, trying to laugh off the incident not too successfully.

"Oh for God's sake, John! For once in your life, try to be serious," Miguel argued angrily.

"I don't see any point in making the incident something more than it was," John retaliated. "You're trying to turn this thing into a big mystery."

"Juanillo," la señora said softly, "*no seas pesado.* Unless we know either the who or the why of this matter, we shall not rest easy. If it was merely a prank, it was a very dangerous one. The intent was not one of nuisance value, but deadly malice . . . if that is all that it was. We must find out who did this, and levity is no way to handle it."

John's mouth set in a hard line. Crossing over to where Jeannine was sitting he rested a hand on her shoulder. "Yes, I agree, Doña Josefina, but Miguel's scowl and secretiveness is only frightening Jeannie needlessly. He's making it all sound as if there's some dark plot against me, some phantom conspiracy."

Miguel's expression softened only for a moment as he said, "Or worse, perhaps it is Jeannine who is in danger."

The ease with which Miguel had redirected the danger struck Jeannine like a blow. Had he deliberately set out to undermine her recovery, he could not have sabotaged it more forcefully. She reacted to his comment, and the way he'd delivered it, with a quickened pulse and an insecurity bordering on paranoia. Fleetingly, an evil tableau displayed itself within her mind, an image of her good friend Dr. Sternig sending her off to this remote locale, to la señora, a mastermind of evil, with Miguel and John her pawns in a malevolent ritual. It was silly, of course, and the vision burst almost as rapidly as it had formed. But she could not quite forgive Miguel, or understand his motive for introducing such a threat. Why would anyone have any interest in her, she reasoned. After all, she was merely the hired help. The only person who could possibly care whether she was there or not was Señora de Lorca — and all she had to do, to get rid of Jeannine, was fire her. No. The whole idea was ludicrous. Miguel couldn't possibly resent her presence; she had certainly been staying out of his way, not interfering with him or his life. And her intelligence once again denied the possibility that she was the target — if, indeed, a target existed at all. John was probably right. Some hostile teenager, on drugs perhaps. And the more she rationalized that there was no planned threat to any of them, the greater her resentment toward Miguel became. Why had he said such a terrible thing? Was he deliberately trying to frighten her? But why? What on earth for? It made no sense!

While the air still hung heavy with their individual unspoken speculations, Chata entered the room and whispered something to la señora. The old woman nodded, took a deep breath, and rose to her feet. "You may all go into lunch now, I'll join you in a moment."

"Where are you going, Doña Josefina," Miguel demanded.

She glanced at him with such total disdain for his impudence that Miguel could only accede to her wish for privacy. As the three of them silently filed into the dining room, Jeannine couldn't help but note that la señora was headed toward the small receiving salon just off the entry hall, where unexpected visitors were taken while waiting to be received. Briefly, Jeannine wondered who would have the temerity to call, unannounced, at lunchtime; yet by the time they were seated, John was diverting her with suggestions of how they might spend the afternoon together.

Miguel picked at his food in silence, and la señora did not join them until coffee was being served. Jeannine could not imagine what sort of business would have detained the woman for so long, and especially at mealtime — which la señora held as among the most important events of any day. Faintly, Jeannine heard a car engine start up and the sound of tires rolling across the gravel in the driveway at the side of the house. Who would come to the side entrance? Why not the front door? And suddenly Jeannine remembered what Miguel had said after their first breakfast: "I hope you have not come to the wrong place . . . for your sake, I hope not."

When Jeannine and John returned from their swim, it was already quite chilly and the sun hovered over the ocean's horizon like a crimson balloon. John had borrowed la señora's vintage Cadillac pending the repair of his own car, and giggling like children they discussed the old woman's refusal to purchase a newer car. According to John, she kept the car mostly to please Manuel, who apparently had developed a fondness for the monstrous limousine that bordered on a fetish. Manuel, it seemed, spent every spare moment keeping the car in perfect condition, washing it personally instead of taking it to any of the carwashes in nearby Monterey, and never permitting any *gringo* mechanic to touch it — only Manuel ever worked on the car's engine, keeping it constantly in perfect mechanical condition. And even though it was somewhat unkind, both John and Jeannine confessed that they found hilarious the image of small, wiry Manuel with his chauffeur's cap maneuvering the huge, hearse-like vehicle with such dignity and unabashed pride. Neither of them doubted for a moment that la señora would will the vehicle to Manuel upon her death. The subject of her death sobered them both; it was too close at hand, too much of a possibility for either of them to be able to laugh.

Yet, when they pulled up in front of the house, both of them had to smile at Manuel magically appearing to take the car to the garage — doubtless to inspect it for damage, or remove some speck of lint upon its leather interior.

John heard it first. Even as his hand rested upon the doorknob of the massive front door, he paused and sent a surprised look at Jeannine. "Hear that?"

"Hear what?" she said, and then discerned the muffled sounds of what could only be barking dogs. "Where did they come from?" she wondered aloud, not expecting an answer.

John opened the door and neither of them was prepared for what charged at them. As if the hounds of hell had been unleashed, two huge German shepherds thundered across the tiled foyer, snarling and growling with such ferocity that the sound would have struck terror in the Devil himself. John barely had time to pull the door shut again, and was perspiring freely as he pulled himself together. They both listened to the continued barking and snarling, and the powerful paws scratching on the door.

Seconds later, Miguel's footsteps resounded on the tiles, his voice gave a series of harsh commands to the beasts. And then there was silence. Utter silence. John looked apprehensively at Jeannine, and she herself had a moment's fear that Miguel had been ripped apart by the dogs. But then the front door opened, and Miguel motioned them both to enter. The two dogs were then seated like mantelpiece decorations; tense and ready to spring to attack, if necessary, but apparently they were obedient to Miguel.

"Come in, it's all right now. I'll have to introduce you to the dogs so this won't happen again."

John stepped across the threshold, not too subtly keeping a safe distance from the dogs. "Where in hell did they come from?" he asked in a voice that implied Miguel had probably conjured them.

Miguel smiled at Jeannine and extended his hand to her. "It's all right," he said. "Here, give me your scarf and I'll give the dogs your scent so they will recognize you in the future."

Jeannine hesitated only for a second, but Miguel's eyes were so warm, so reassuring, that she complied. He took the scarf and held it before the dogs, saying "friend" several times and patting their heads. "Come

94

pet them, Jeannine, so they will recognize you as a friend."

"Are you sure . . ." she asked.

"Yes, yes. Come now, don't be afraid."

She gingerly approached them and Miguel introduced her to Hans and Bruno, nodding to her to pet them while he did so. Hans seemed to endure her touch and her mere existence, while Bruno growled briefly at first, then began to lick her hand.

"What about me?" John asked.

Miguel laughed. "I'm not so terribly sure that you *are* a friend."

"Now look here, Mike!"

"I was only joking, John. Give me your jacket or something to hold to their noses."

While the introduction was being made, John once again asked why the dogs were there, uncertainly patting their proud heads.

"I bought them this afternoon, at that obedience school in Monterey. If anyone is up to foul play, they'll not come around the house to practice it. No one who hasn't been accepted by these dogs will come near the place!"

He said it with such determination, such complete assurance, that it frightened Jeannine. There was an aura of cruelty about Miguel that she found terribly disturbing. But summoning all her courage, she attempted to coax Bruno to come to her; the dog did not budge.

"He will only obey my commands, Jeannine. They'll be friendly to you, of course, but they will not obey you useless it's something they are supposed to do in the first place. These animals have been trained as guard dogs, not pets. They're usually sold to businesses or industries to accompany the watchman. I had wanted to get Dobermans, but Doña Josefina wouldn't hear of it." He laughed lightly, almost sardonically. "She said that the shepherds were bad enough, but that Dobermans terrify her."

"I didn't think anything would frighten her!" John said. Turning his back on the dogs, he hurried to the living room and fixed himself a drink. "Where is the old lady, anyway?" he called to Miguel.

Jeannine was slightly taken aback. Somehow, calling la señora "the old lady" just seemed terribly shallow and in extremely poor taste. But she knew how fond John was of la señora and immediately assumed that he was using the term affectionately.

"She's changing for dinner," Miguel replied, taking Jeannine by the elbow and escorting her into the living room.

The unexpected physical contact caused Jeannine to react involuntarily with a start.

There was something so vital about Miguel's touch, almost mystically charged, that she found herself somewhat light-headed. If Miguel had noticed it, he was not revealing it, and she swiftly dismissed the reaction, attributing it to the excitement of the day, to the shock of finding two vicious dogs in the house. By the time John handed her the martini, she'd put the matter out of her mind.

Chapter 8

"The biota of the Carmel Valley, and its environs, will not tolerate the biological magnification of your industry. Your wastes are jeopardizing eutrophication, and my committee will take immediate measures if you do not voluntarily remedy the situation." La señora paused in her dictation, giving Jeannine a chance to get it all down. While no one could say that la señora was actually pacing the room while dictating, she nonetheless was standing, resting upon her cane, except when she used it to tap on the floor by way of some inner punctuation.

It was not at all unusual for Doña Josefina to ask Jeannine to work in the evening, after dinner. Often, the woman could spend an entire afternoon with her environmental committee, discussing and planning and organizing; then, when she came home, she would take a restful nap, have supper, and dictate a few letters — or, as Jeannine had come to call them privately, threatening notes. It had not taken Jeannine long to become accustomed to such terms and phrases as trophic level, symbiosis, or renewable resources, and she had quickly devised her own shorthand symbols for them.

Not once had la señora ever dictated what Jeannine would consider a cordial letter, or even just a polite one. When la señora got down to business, she was *all* business — virtually ruthless in her venerable position within the community. Even when corresponding to some chairman of the board, la señora's tone was designed to reduce him to mush, to make him feel like some retarded schoolboy playing at grown-up games.

Even the most innocent of letters, social matters, were dictated with all the warmth and graciousness of an order from General Patton in the heat of battle. Jeannine's favorite of these had been six invitations to be sent to local Carmel officials: *I shall be receiving at four, this Saturday, the 21st of May. Tea shall be served promptly.* A death notice would have been softer.

Initially, Jeannine had attempted to temper the woman's dictation when she typed up the correspondence. However, she had abandoned any such effort in short order. At first, la señora would merely scratch through Jeannine's rewriting, refusing to sign such tripe, forcing Jeannine to retype the letters. But after the fourth or fifth time, la señora simply sat back in her cane desk chair, and summoned Jeannine to the side of her desk.

"My dear child," she began with an icy edge in her voice. "If I dictate that I am an old woman, I do not expect you to rephrase my words to indicate that I am no longer as young as I used to be. If I say that the sea is a cerulean blue, I do not wish to have you alter the color to turquoise. And if I call someone an idiot or a fool, I will not stand for you watering down my words to a mere slap on the wrist. The word dictate does not merely mean the taking down of a letter. . . it is also a command."

Jeannine did not dare offer any contradiction, but she did feel that her own side of the story was in order. "I'm accustomed to revising the letters of extremely busy people, people who are merely giving me the gist of their thoughts. . . ."

The woman's cane came down sharply on the floor. "I do not deal in gists! I say precisely what I wish to say!"

"Certainly, Mrs. de Lorca, I had not meant to presume," Jeannine responded.

"Well, you have. Precisely that. And I shall not stand for it."

"Of course, Mrs. de Lorca." And the matter was closed . . . except, as Jeannine noted with an inner smile, the woman often tempered her own letters thereafter. And, on a few occasions, she had even interrupted herself to ask Jeannine if she were being too imperious.

Somehow, tonight Jeannine felt that there was something very amiss about la señora's attitude during the dictation. They were both, to be sure, very aware of the dogs sleeping warily in the corner of the den; but even so, there was something about the woman's tone that was unlike her. She seemed to be rushing, as if she had very little time and were feeling the pressure of an insurmountable amount of work within an impossible deadline. There was a tension in the room, a tautness to the woman's voice, that set Jeannine on edge. Finally, la señora indicated the usual signature for the letter and Jeannine crossed to her own desk with the huge IBM typewriter where she sat for a second just staring out the window.

The moonlight cast a grayish halo about the trees and shrubs, and the wind teased the leaves into a chorale of whispers. Beyond the grounds, down through the ravines and crevices of the mountain, Carmel-by-the-Sea glittered faintly in the distance. The vista was serene. Nature remained untouched, unconcerned, with the emotional dramas of the transient humans. Beyond Carmel, the ocean relaxed with a gentler tide, its unfathomable blackness disturbed only by a wedge of blue-gray across the surface as it reflected the moon's reign. All creatures slept in peace, all the world was in order. Except at "Puerta de Paz.". . .

So engrossed was Jeannine in her revery that she had not noticed la señora coming to stand beside her and share the moment. *"Capa que cubre todos los humanos pensamientos,"* the woman said softly. "Cervantes referred to sleep, but I think he would not mind if I stretched it to include the beauty of nature."

"What does it mean?" Jeannine asked. It was a moment of closeness that she would probably never forget, of shared spirituality rooted in mutual appreciation and respect for the omniscience of nature.

"It is a phrase I think of often," la señora said, and rested her fragile hand upon Jeannine's young shoulder. " 'The mantle that covers all human thoughts.' I think that beauty is also a mantle; it is a comfort to the soul, a reassurance that ugliness is, after all, only something created by man. There are times, *niña,* when I think that civilization is a pity . . . we have lost much because of it."

102

Jeannine only nodded to the woman's statement. Yes, civilization had given much to humanity — the arts, of course, and medicine, and technology. But the price was high. The sense of identity, of simplicity, of oneness — gone. She wondered if one had to be somewhat corrupted before appreciation could exist. Had the Costanoans appreciated the beauty of the area any more than la señora; or perhaps, in their uneducated simplicity, they had enjoyed it less . . . taken it for granted. It was a moot question, she knew.

She felt la señora remove her hand and turn her back to the window. The movement filled Jeannine with an apprehension similar to the dead stillness before a storm; a kind of compressed, instinctive reaction of suspense and fear of the unknown.

"I would appreciate it, Jeannine, if you would not see Aaron Franklin again."

Jeannine twisted in her chair; her surprise at the woman knowing about the chance meeting showed clearly on her face.

"Yes, I know. You think it was an accidental meeting. It wasn't. There are things happening in this house that are the business of no one, and I would not wish them discussed. Aaron Franklin has a morbid curiosity about us. In his mind, perhaps he feels his interest is justified. But I do not approve of it."

"But I would never dream of discussing your affairs with Dr. Franklin!" Jeannine protested, somewhat offended by Doña Josefina's lack of trust in her judgment.

"You might not think you are saying anything revealing, *niña,* but Aaron Franklin is not quite the good, small-town doctor that you think he is. I do not wish to be unreasonable, and this is not an arbitrary request. I have my own reasons for asking you not to associate with him."

Resentment boiled up in Jeannine. "Señora, I am your employee, and I do not wish to seem rude or disrespectful . . . but don't you think that what I do in my free time is my business?"

La señora's somber dark eyes studied Jeannine for a moment. "I am not asking you to be rude to him, only not to seek out his company."

"And if he seeks mine?"

The woman shrugged her frail shoulders. "I see I have turned you into a Pandora with my wish. *Qué lástima.* Well, it is my own fault."

Jeannine instantly relented and much as she would have liked to go to the woman, to hug her affectionately and reassure her,

104

la señora's bearing would not permit such a familiarity. Yet, a part of her was still smarting from the woman's attitude about whom she might see and when. "I promise you I shall never say anything to Dr. Franklin that wouldn't meet with your approval."

Doña Josefina sighed lightly. "I fear I asked too much of you, *niña*. You are young, and full of independence, and cannot be treated like a Spanish daughter in the eighteenth century. Let us not speak of it again. You will do what you must, and I am a meddlesome old woman too accustomed to dominating others."

There was nothing Jeannine could say in reply that would not have resulted in her capitulation to the woman's wishes; or worse, have indicated her agreement to la señora's analysis. It was best to say nothing; but Jeannine could not help wishing the subject had never come up. It had placed a willful veil between them.

As she lay in bed, later that night, Jeannine tossed uncomfortably in her sleep. Vague dreams of a threatening nature plagued her sleep. It was more the mood of the dreams than any actual envisioned person or endangering situation. But at one point, she awoke with a start and found her heart pounding as if she had been running and running to escape. To escape — what? Childish imaginings, she chided herself. Simply a nightmare of some sort, too nebulous even to be recalled. She decided to slip down to the kitchen and prepare some warm milk and honey for herself before trying to go back to sleep. Childish or not, she knew she would have to calm down before a restful sleep would come.

Throwing off the pastel-print quilt, she slid into her slippers and pulled on her emerald green robe. She reached up automatically to flip her shoulder length auburn hair free from the robe's collar before opening the door. The house was very old, and the floors creaked even on the main floor, but upstairs they seemed to conspire against silence; no matter how hard she tried, every tiptoed step caused a squeak or groan to some degree. Jeannine only hoped that the sounds did not carry too far in the quiet of the night. So she opened her bedroom door carefully, avoiding any gesture that would create even more noise. Then she stepped out into the hallway and made her way toward the stairs.

She'd noted the very first night of her arrival that there was another stairway, one that led up yet another flight from the second floor. Fortunately, she'd not had to display any unseemly curiosity; Chata had volunteered the information that they led to a vast attic-type of storeroom. However, as Jeannine neared the steps, she noticed that there was a light coming from beneath the attic door. She wondered if she'd ever seen it before; if perhaps it was not a light left on continuously — but she'd never seen a light on the third floor from outside, and the darkened hallway had never revealed its presence before.

Hesitating at the top of the stairs, Jeannine became aware of voices from the attic; angry, harsh voices. Masculine voices.

"You've never given me a chance . . . not ever!"

"A chance at what? A chance to kill the old woman with the truth?"

"You're so damned smug, aren't you? You know what's in her will, know it by memory. Nothing worries you, does it. But I've got a right to know, too. I've got a right. . . ."

"You've got the same rights I do, but even if I knew what was in the will, it would be accidentally, and not something to be shared like some locker room anecdote!"

Jeannine could barely distinguish the words, only dimly recognize the voices —

but not enough to be totally certain. Both voices were so constricted with anger and frustration, they were very difficult to establish. It could have been Manuel and Dr. Franklin, for all she knew — or John and Miguel, at each other's throats once again. But whoever they were, she knew it was none of her business, knew that it had nothing to do with her. Consequently, she resumed her descent. But as she put her weight on the first tile of the stairway, it gave beneath her and she went tumbling face forward down the stairs.

Chapter 9

The fall had only knocked the breath out of her, and in no time, Jeannine had recovered consciousness. She was beginning to feel that someone had written a very bad script in the old Keystone Kops tradition. Every time she turned around, she was recovering from something or another. It was becoming ludicrous; she was not cut out for the simpering life of the fragile female personality, the type of woman who was constantly taking to her bed with the vapors or sinking spells.

As she opened her eyes, she heard Miguel saying, "Thank God!" and his strong arms lifting her up, carrying her up the stairs to her room. Gently, he lowered her to her bed, softly saying something to himself in Spanish, which she could not comprehend. Jeannine was not familiar enough with Miguel that she could interpret his thoughts by his tone of voice. He could have been cursing her clumsiness as well as giving thanks for her well-being. But shortly after Miguel had her tucked in, her addled senses perceived a depression at the foot of her bed.

Jeannine looked down and saw Mrs. de Lorca, draped in a brocaded lounging robe that looked too heavy for her petite frame to support. "Well, *niña,* are you making accidents some sort of habit?"

"Doña Josefina!" Miguel chided.

But Jeannine laughed. It certainly did look that way, and she fully understood just how the señora had meant it. "I hope not," she answered.

Miguel cleared his throat pointedly. "I'll have a look at that step first thing in the morning," he said.

"Ay, Miguel, you're not going to start all that all over again, are you?"

"*Pero, Doña Josefina, dos veces dentro de un mes?*"

La señora *tsk*ed her exasperation. "Since when is there a timetable for accidents?"

Jeannine had been about to say something to stop them from entering into yet another bickering session when Chata appeared with a tray bearing three mugs of steaming hot cocoa, plus three snifters of cognac. "*Gracias,* Chata," la señora said, and indicated that she place the tray on the nightstand next to Jeannine. She wondered, of course, where John was during all this commotion, and then realized that there had not been that much noise, and that doubtlessly he had slept right through her fall. Certainly if he had known about it, he would have come to her aid instantly, and it would probably have been he who had carried her upstairs.

Which meant, disturbingly, that Miguel had been one of the men in heated argument up in the attic . . . and John had not. How else could Miguel have been at her side so quickly, and why else would John not be present? But then, Doña Josefina, with her very deep voice, could have been the other party in the attic. She too was up and immediately on hand. It was almost as if they had expected something like this to happen, as if they'd been waiting for it. . . . But why? To what purpose? None of it was making any sense at all!

The following Sunday, Jeannine asked la señora if she could accompany her to Mass. Though she had been to visit Mission San Carlos Borromeo before, it had been in the midst of some conducted tour with all sorts of non-Catholic people gaping at the altar sarcophagus of its founder, Padre Junípero Serra. She had felt like an interloper, under those circumstances, and had been wanting to attend Mass at the mission when there were no gawking tourists.

La señora seemed pleased at her request, and gently reminded her that all ladies must wear a head-covering inside the church. It was not a problem for Jeannine; she deplored hats, but was very fond of wearing scarves to keep her red hair safe from the playful winds of the area.

Manuel drove them to nine o'clock Mass, with Chata at his side up in front, dressed in her Sunday best. Quietly, the local residents gathered before the entrance inside the walled grounds, milling about the courtyard gardens and chatting amiably before entering for High Mass. Although many had already entered the church, Jeannine and la señora, trailed by Chata and Manuel, waited until the last moment, enjoying the warm morning sun upon their faces. The unusual spring weather had prompted the climbing rose vines along the adobe walls of the mission to burst with color, and with no difficulty at all, Jeannine could envision the mission as it must have been originally. There was something reassuring, comforting, about being able to walk upon the same ground as the early settlers of California; it gave her a sense of continuity that defied death and man's transient hours. She thought of the thousands of Indians who had been converted at this very spot, been baptized within those walls, and who had worked willingly to aid the padres to build their monument to God.

Jeannine had read about the mission and Father Serra; how he had left his mission in neighboring Monterey because the Indians were so frightened of the Spanish soldiers there; and together, Father Serra and his Indian friends laboriously erected their own mission on the banks of the Carmel River, near the ocean.

At a nod from la señora, Chata and Manuel preceded them into the church. Incense hung heavily in the air as they crossed the uneven tile floor, and Jeannine couldn't help shivering a little at the change of temperature within the thick adobe walls. Simple wooden benches constituted the pews, and while the altar was not nearly so elaborate as many that Jeannine had seen, its gilt facade and somewhat primitive figurines showed the love and tenderness that had gone into its making in 1770.

It was as if Jeannine had somehow crossed a time zone. Even though she was not a Catholic, there was a sense of tranquillity and devotion here during Mass which she had never witnessed in any of the major cathedrals in metropolitan areas; here there was simplicity and harmony. Even the

113

stations of the cross were unusual; instead of bas-relief representations, or sculpture, there were oil paintings darkened with age and cracked. It would not have surprised Jeannine in the least if the doors had been thrown open, admitting Spanish soldiers to round up Indians as labor conscripts.

As they all filed out after Mass, la señora paused to thank the priest for the sermon. Jeannine excused herself to stroll through the gardens. When she neared the fountain, she was momentarily surprised to see Aaron Franklin seated on its rim. "I didn't know you were a Catholic, Dr. Franklin," she said, smiling warmly at his benevolent expression.

"I'm about as Catholic as you are, Jeannine," he said, patting the spot next to him for her to join him. "I come here occasionally, mostly for the ritual of it all, I suppose. How're the bruises coming along?"

"Oh, fine. But I'm such a clod. You wouldn't believe the fall I took the other night — headfirst down the stairs. Miguel said there was a loose tile, or something."

Dr. Franklin looked at her sharply. "A loose tile at 'Puerta de Paz'? Not likely!"

"Well, it's an old house, after all."

He shook his head slowly, puffing at his pipe. "First the auto accident, and now a

114

loose tile. No, my dear, it's too much of a coincidence."

Not knowing what to say, Jeannine said nothing. She felt very uncomfortable running into Dr. Franklin with la señora probably wondering where she was. It was an awkward enough situation now that Doña Josefina had specifically asked her to avoid the man. And even as those thoughts entered her mind, she observed señora de Lorca approaching them and then stopping short as she recognized Dr. Franklin.

"I must be going," Jeannine said with a nod in la señora's direction.

Dr. Franklin smiled, almost ruefully. "Perhaps you should think about really going," he said. "It might be a good idea if you were to get away from Carmel altogether."

Refusing to be drawn into a conversation about some nebulous lurking "danger," Jeannine merely waved and briskly walked up to join the others. The four of them walked in silence back to the gleaming Cadillac, and it wasn't until they were on their way back to the hacienda that la señora said a word to Jeannine.

"And now he follows you."

Jeannine knew better than to try to defend the old gentleman but she did offer his excuse. "He wasn't following me, señora. He said he comes to Mass on occasion."

Doña Josefina snorted imperiously. "The last occasion had to be ten years ago!"

Without warning, Jeannine's sense of justice and fair play rose to the surface. "I don't know why you no longer consider Dr. Franklin your friend, but I'm not enjoying the role of a pawn between you!"

Mrs. de Lorca stiffened. "A pawn? What are you talking about?"

"You tell me to stay away from him, not to talk to him . . . and today he suggested that my accidents might not be so accidental, that perhaps I should leave Carmel. Since no one will tell me what any of this is all about, I'm getting a little annoyed with all this heavy mystery."

La señora's expression softened, her eyes revealing a weary patience. "How like youth to think itself the center of the universe. No, *niña,* you are merely someone new to the hacienda, someone who can be pumped for information. I don't know why Aaron would suggest that you leave here — unless he is striving for dramatic effect. As for the accidents, we already know that one was quite premeditated and deliberate. *Why* is the question."

She paused to lean forward and rap on the glass partition, gesturing to Manuel to speed up, then sat back heavily. "That man," she said. "He'd ride a horse into a deadly lather, but his precious Cadillac cannot be driven over ten miles per hour!"

"Well whatever the reasons — you saying push and Dr. Franklin saying pull — it's putting me in a position that's far from amusing."

The fragile old woman's hand patted Jeannine's. "You are upsetting yourself for nothing, *niña*. Aaron and I are old people, having an old people's quarrel that will last until one of us has died. We do not see things in the same light. Sadly, Aaron functions best in an aura of secrecy and intrigue; he thinks that espionage is the only way to subvert me. It is not for you to worry about such things."

Jeannine made no reply and they rode to the hacienda in silence. Nonetheless, she could not quite agree with la señora about Dr. Franklin. He had always seemed quite open and candid with her, while Mrs. de Lorca's intentions often seemed shrouded in mysterious innuendoes and shadowy inferences. It was Mrs. de Lorca who was fighting the world, holding high court against the princes of industry and their kingdoms of mechanized progress. Whereas Aaron Franklin was a mellowed, retired physician, living in spartan simplicity, who went about his business, and didn't seem to interfere in the lives of others. There had been his remark to her about leaving Carmel, but Jeannine felt that it was the sort of remark a friend might make, advice to avoid a possibly sticky situation before she could become a catalyst. Jeannine had not taken his remark as meddling manipulation, but simply as one of concern.

And what old people's quarrel did la señora mean? Some ancient feud between them of the trivial he-said she-said variety? Why couldn't Mrs. de Lorca just come out and say what it was that stood between them? Something akin to, "Look, I caught that man stealing flowers from my garden and I've not spoken to him since!" If the entire matter were truly so unimportant, then why was la señora still not explaining it? It occurred to Jeannine that she might ask Miguel about it, yet she was relatively certain that all she'd get from him would be a deep mumble and a scowl. No. Perhaps she should ask John. He spent a great deal of time at "Puerta de Paz"; it was quite likely that he would know what it was all about. She resolved to do so that very day, at her first opportunity to be with John alone — away from the influences of the house and its occupants. And if John didn't know? Perhaps Olga . . . but no, Olga didn't have a heart for intrigue. If you told Olga, "It's a secret!" Olga would forget and repeat the whole thing to the next person she ran into.

Jeannine realized for the first time how much she resented secretive people. They made life so much more complicated than it already was. . . .

Chapter 10

Later that afternoon Jeannine found an opportunity to talk to John in privacy. A housing development company had been negotiating to buy up a considerable number of acres in the Carmel Valley, and la señora was fighting it with all the fury of a lioness protecting her cubs. There was to be a meeting of the principals involved in the dispute up at the Asilomar Conference Grounds, and Doña Josefina was taking Miguel as her legal counselor.

Jeannine knew that Miguel represented his grandmother on many of these occasions, and she had always marveled at how he found the time. His regular practice was in Monterey, and while he usually only spoke about his more interesting "important" clients in the broadest noncommittal way, on occasion he would refer to some horrendous injustice being done to a client who invariably turned out to be a migrant farm worker or factory employee of Mexican-American heritage. It sometimes seemed to Jeannine that Miguel only took on the monied clients in order to support the work he did for the Chicano community. Since she found it nearly impossible to think of Miguel as the kindly family attorney, benevolently administering advice to the poor, she assumed that Miguel's furious interest was based on principle, rather than pure chauvinism.

In fact, sometimes she wondered if Miguel didn't suffer from a feudal-lord complex. He would occasionally refer to some client as *"el pobre peon"* as if these people could not survive without his guidance. Usually, Miguel's attitude amused her, providing her with insights into the workings of his mind. She found it rather touching that Miguel could become so violently upset over cases that would not earn him a dime. At other times, however, she felt that his attitude was a trifle patronizing, and she had to bite her lip to keep still. Normally, if not always, Miguel's comments or explanations were never directed to her, but to la señora during mealtime. He was not seeking *her* approval or opinion, but his grandmother's.

But today she refused to be concerned about such things; she was determined to learn the truth of the Franklin-de Lorca feud from easygoing John. As soon as

Miguel and his grandmother had left the hacienda, Jeannine asked John if he would like to join her in a leisurely stroll. John accepted her invitation with a teasing "It's not often you ask me to go along!"

In the hall, they sidestepped the dogs, who reared their heads menacingly as they passed, and walked out into the late afternoon sunshine. Off in the distance, they could see the fog beginning to build over the valley, enshrouding the mountaintops in gray tumbling mist. To the west, the ocean shimmered with golden sequins as the sun descended toward the horizon. There wasn't an hour of any day or night when Jeannine could not find some spectacular aspect of nature. While the village of Carmel was quite charming on its own, the locale of the hacienda afforded breathtaking beauty from every point on the compass. At moments like these, Jeannine couldn't help wondering if the Garden of Eden had not been at that spot in California; perhaps, somewhere in the world, there might be another place equally beautiful . . . but not more beautiful.

John slowly walked behind Jeannine. They had been walking along the mountain footpath in silence since leaving the house until they crested a wild poppy field and stood looking southward. In the distance, carefully hoed fields appeared, with miniscule barn-red shacks or houses discernible.

"What's that?" Jeannine asked, waiting for her reply as John lighted a cigarette.

"Artichoke fields," he answered, smiling down at her. "You certainly are a city girl, aren't you." He said it lightly, teasing her gently. "See those black specks over there, away from the fields, up that slope? Those, my young city girl, are nothing less than Black Angus cows!"

"How could you stand to move away, John . . . how can you live in San Francisco when all this beauty is right here?"

John shrugged. "There's a different kind of beauty in San Francisco. There's nightlife and fun, parties and nightclubs, people to see, places to go. I like to come down here to see Grandmother, but I couldn't stand it for very long."

They sat down side by side on the tall green grass and took in the horizon. Jeannine's own awe served to diminish John's obviously unimpressed attitude toward their environs. "No, let Doña Josefina and Miguel get into all the conservation squabbles; it's nothing I really care about. Put a polo field out there, or build a country club, and then maybe you'd get my interest stirred up. It's only a matter of time before this whole area will be overrun with housing tracts and condominiums, with factories and parking lots. I guess Miguel's interest is mostly to keep things status quo for as long as Doña Josefina is still alive. . . ."

"Is that so terrible?" Jeannine asked, rather surprised by John's lackadaisical attitude.

"No, I suppose not. It's his life. But I think that one of the advantages to getting old is the ability to face reality . . . and Grandmother is not facing it. On the other hand," he said, laughing boyishly, "it's probably the only thing that's keeping her alive. She really believes she can keep big business away from her doorstep by wielding her cane in matriarchal outrage. I suppose you think I'm being callous and cruel?"

Jeannine smiled noncommittally. "No, I guess not. You're facing facts, I guess. It's just that I'm a romantic. If I'd been born and raised here, I think I'd put up a pretty gigantic struggle to keep the natural beauty of my home."

John stubbed out his cigarette and lit another. "Well, that's all well and good, but you can't eat natural beauty. Industry means jobs, and jobs support families. Romantics complain about our welfare programs, but they won't budge an inch to create new businesses so people can work."

"Surely that's not the only way to help people in need," Jeannine said, taken aback. "We could tear down the tenements, the ghettoes, and put up factories there instead . . . then people could afford to move to the suburbs and raise their children in clean air and safe neighborhoods."

He grinned impishly and took her hand. "You're beginning to sound like la señora."

She had to admit it was true. She'd not really given much thought to such things before coming to Carmel; the lives of other people had always remained separate and apart from her own. It was not apathy so much as being uninformed and, therefore, uninvolved. Living with la señora, getting caught up in her fight to preserve the area, had wrought subtle changes in her consciousness, Jeannine realized. John's comment also provided her with a perfect opening to inquire about Dr. Franklin.

"John?"

"Hmm?"

"Why does Doña Josefina dislike Dr. Franklin so much?"

The expression on his face clouded only momentarily. "Oh, I don't know. Some old feud between them."

Jeannine persisted. "Yet when we were in that auto accident, she telephoned him. I remember she even defended him to Dr. Ortíz. Don't you think that's a little odd?"

"Not really. A doctor's a doctor. Old Franklin was the only one available at the time. As for defending him to Ortíz, well, she's not so fond of Ortíz either. Maybe she just has a thing against all doctors."

Jeannine shook her head. "No, it's more than that. Are you aware of the fact that she asked me to avoid Dr. Franklin, not to speak to him? She truly thinks of him as a threat of some sort."

"Maybe he pinched her in the old days!"

"John! That's a terrible thing to say!"

She had no sooner said it when she heard the report of a rifle. As Jeannine turned to see if John had also heard it, she saw that he'd been wounded in the left shoulder. With a cry of alarm, she breathed his name just as he dragged her down flat on the grass.

"Stay down . . . whoever it was is still out there and might try to take another shot."

"But your shoulder . . ." she whispered.

"I don't think it's too serious . . . hurts like hell, though."

"John, you're bleeding badly! We've got

to get you back to the house!"

John considered her suggestion, gazing from her concerned face down to the flow of blood through his shirt. His face had paled considerably, and beads of perspiration were already forming on his forehead. He looked more frightened than in pain, and Jeannine could certainly understand that. "All right," he said, "you'll make better time alone than if we try to get back together. Stay low in the grass till you're over the crest and out of sight . . . then . . ." He winced as he shifted his position. "Then get Miguel and bring him back out here. He's big enough to sling me over his shoulder. There are times," he joked feebly, "when it pays to have a bull for a cousin."

But Jeannine had already begun to scramble up the hillside, worried that John might bleed to death if he didn't receive medical attention immediately.

It seemed endless hours before she reached the house, and not till she was inside did she remember that Miguel was not at home, and probably wouldn't be for quite some time. With a mounting sense of panic, her pulse pounding in her head, she ran to the kitchen and breathlessly explained what had happened to Manuel and Chata. To her enormous relief, Manuel took over command instantly, barking orders to Chata to telephone *el doctor Ortíz*. He swiftly went to the linen closet and took out a heavy brocaded tablecloth, tucked it carefully under his arm, and then motioned to Jeannine that she should lead him back to John.

"Perhaps I am not strong enough to lift Don Juanillo, but I can drag him to safety across the hill and to the footpath. Not to concern yourself, señorita Wellman, I will get him home safely!"

And somehow Jeannine knew that Manuel would. He had a look of determination she'd not seen — nor thought about — since the few months she'd spent at the orphanage before her aunt took custody of her. There was an incredible strength born out of desperation; Jeannine had seen that expression too often at the impressionable age of eight to have forgotten it completely.

They left together, wordlessly, rushing up the path to the fading sounds of Chata's frantic explanation to the doctor's office. Manuel did not ask why or who or how; it had happened, and there was no time for senseless questions. Someone had tried to kill John, and he needed help.

But Jeannine's mind was racing with unresolved questions. It was John's car that had been tampered with, and now this. As for the loosened tile, perhaps that, too, had been done deliberately, on the chance that John would be the first to use the stairs. But even as her brain struggled with these possibilities, the question of why kept recurring.

The return to where John lay seemed to take only seconds, but when they reached him, he was unconscious. Manuel stooped down and concentrated on taking John's pulse. Jeannine's own pulse seemed to be pounding harder, as if pumping blood for two, while she stood helplessly watching.

"Don Juanillo is all right," Manuel said. "He has fainted. Perhaps from the loss of blood. *No se preocupa, señorita,* he will be all right. I promise you that."

Together they made a litter from the tablecloth and rolled John onto it as carefully as they could. She began to lift the foot end, but Manuel shook his head. "We will need your strength when we reach the footpath . . . here the grass is soft and he will slide easily."

She followed in their path, feeling useless and incompetent until they reached the other side, beyond the poppies, and there Manuel paused while she got a good grip on the tablecloth. John's deadweight was too much for her, and the tablecloth kept slipping from her hands, causing them to have to stop and let her get a new hold. Finally, it occurred to her that it would be far simpler if she just grabbed hold of John's ankles and forgot about the makeshift litter. It worked far more efficiently and they made a speedy return to the hacienda, where Dr. Ortíz was awaiting them.

As soon as they had stretched John out upon his bed the doctor turned to Jeannine and ordered her to go and lie down. He also instructed Chata to take her a stiff brandy and a glass of water so Jeannine could take her medication at once.

Chata took Jeannine's elbow and led her to her own room. Once inside, Jeannine's heart began to pound in her ears, and the room turned a dull yellow, as if she were about to faint. Chata helped her to her bed, and realizing that Jeannine was shivering, she pulled the coverlet atop her before rushing off to follow the doctor's orders.

Lightheaded, a sense of inner fluttering coursing throughout her body, Jeannine desperately tried to reach her pills, planning to take them even without the benefit of water. Her eyes felt wild and staring, her limbs heavy yet somehow devoid of sensation, as if she were floating, and there was a muted, constant hum within her skull. She pulled open the nightstand drawer and extracted the small plastic receptacle, removed the white cap with fingers made of lead, and was suddenly seized with a gripping, piercing pain in her chest that caused her to let go of the prescription container. Like dried peas, the pills scattered across the thick carpet, and Jeannine broke into wrenching, frightened, sobbing tears.

Chapter 11

"The time has come to call in the police!" Miguel argued. "There's a connection between these so-called accidents. The crash was not some prankster's jealous action, and the loosened tile was done deliberately as well — there were chips out of the tile where a knife or chisel had been used. And now this!"

John was propped up on the couch in the living room, obviously enjoying every moment of all this attention. Though la señora listened attentively to Miguel, her eyes were fixed upon Jeannine's pale countenance.

"Yes, and there's Jeannine too. Her whole reason for being here is her health," Miguel continued. "To get *away* from tension and pressure!"

"I'm feeling much better, Miguel, truly I am."

Doña Josefina nodded slowly, her keen eyes appraising the sincerity in Jeannine's expression. "Nonetheless, *niña,* we have sent for your Dr. Sternig."

"You've what?" Jeannine exclaimed in total surprise.

"He's your physician, he knows your entire history. It is best that he examine you after your attack."

John asked, "Why didn't you just send Jeannine back to Los Angeles . . . wouldn't that have been simpler than asking a stranger here . . . we have no examining facilities at 'Puerta de Paz.' "

"We were worried about her making the trip alone. You can't go anywhere with that shoulder of yours, and I have to be here to protect Doña Josefina . . . or you." Miguel crossed the room and poured himself another brandy; then, as an afterthought, asked if anyone else wanted any. John, of course, accepted.

"Moreover," la señora said, "he can use Dr. Ortíz's office for the examination."

Jeannine shuddered. "What bothers me the most, I think, is the realization that there's someone around here who's crazy enough to be a sniper. It was rather like an assassination attempt; something insane, something unhuman . . . here in Carmel. . . ."

"Miguel," la señora said, "get Jeannine another cognac. She's still looking entirely too pale."

Miguel did as he was asked, and when he handed the glass to Jeannine, he rested his other hand on her shoulder in a comforting, concerned manner. The warmth of his flesh burned through her sweater and brought a flush to her face. Aloof or scowling, there was some animal vitality to Miguel's touch that undid Jeannine's reserve like a broken string of pearls. She couldn't explain it; and, given a choice, would have preferred to avoid thinking about it at all.

"Well," John said casually, "sniper or no sniper, the important thing is he's a rotten shot."

"Which gets us right back to calling in the police. This may be nothing more than one of Doña Josefina's enemies trying to throw a scare into her. Arranging little accidents, not caring who gets hurt or how badly. It doesn't have to be someone trying to kill you, John."

"Do you have any enemies, Juanillo?" She asked the question as if she already knew the answer.

John laughed good-naturedly. "Of course I do! Many of them! But I owe them all money, which is why they're enemies, and they're not about to bump me off until I've paid up!"

Incredulously, Jeannine fixed her eyes on

John. Surely he could afford to pay his debts. For that matter, if he couldn't afford it, why did he live such an extravagant life? People who lived beyond their means were always a source of amazement to her; but then, she'd never before known any landed gentry . . . people like John who knew they could get away with anything because someday they would inherit a fortune, and then everything would be all right. To Jeannine, not paying a debt was tantamount to stealing, and people who went about getting out of bills or dodging them were, as far as she was concerned, living in an alien land with a totally different morality.

"*Bueno,*" Doña Josefina sighed, shrugging at John's jocular approach to the subject as if he were only a child, and not to be expected to behave like an adult. "Your 'enemies' want you intact. Mine, on the other hand, want me out of the way; not necessarily dead, but out of the way. Miguel, as we all know, has no enemies other than those he shares through me. Jeannine, what is your community rating?"

"None that I know of," she replied. "I've never been in a position where I could earn any enemies."

"What are you driving at, Doña Josefina?" Miguel wanted to know.

"Only that the police should not be brought into this matter. We are too prominent a family to permit such a newsworthy event . . . it would seem too much like some sordid publicity stunt, and it could set us back months and months in our work to conserve our valley."

"Well, we have to do something!" Miguel rumbled.

"A private detective, perhaps?" Jeannine suggested halfheartedly. She knew la señora would never agree to anything so melodramatic.

La señora closed her eyes momentarily as if in tired contemplation. "Coincidence is not entirely out of the question. Stranger things have happened. However, I have an alternate thought. I propose, Juanillo, that as soon as you are able to travel, you return to San Francisco. And you, Miguel, you should perhaps stay at the hotel in Monterey when Juanillo has left. In that manner, we can narrow down the possible object of these incidents — presupposing there is a target. If someone is trying to bring harm to either of you, it will remove the chances of either Jeannine, or me, becoming innocent victims. However, if these accidents continue to occur here at the hacienda, then I shall send Jeannine back to Los Angeles.

Perhaps then would be the time to consider bringing in the police."

John protested only feebly, and it was clear to everyone in the room that his only reason was that he wouldn't have the opportunity to spend as much time with Jeannine. Miguel, however, was outraged by la señora's plan. "And who would look after you!" he demanded.

La señora smiled slowly. "We do, after all, have Manuel and Chata living here — and there are those awful dogs."

Jeannine's reaction to la señora's plan was one of personal loss. She already felt abandoned and alone, and the observation surprised her. She had not realized how accustomed, how dependent, she had become on having either John or Miguel about the house. Jeannine chastised herself silently; she had accepted a secretarial job with Mrs. de Lorca — she was not, after all, a paid guest in the house. How easy it had been for her to fall into a pattern! Still, she wondered if perhaps she were not being too harsh with herself; she was an emotionally healthy young woman, and who wouldn't enjoy the company of two handsome men? She would have to be made from stone not to react favorably to the situation. She would adjust to living at

"Puerta de Paz" without them; it would be lonely at first, but she would make the transition soon enough.

Jeannine sipped her brandy and observed the de Lorcas discussing their alternatives and possible plans. It struck her as somewhat insensible that no one thought to ask her what she would like to do; whether or not she herself cared to stay on. It seemed that none of them even considered that Jeannine might want to quit and find a "safer" job. Her fate was being discussed between them as a consequence of their own lives, as an extension, but not on a personal level of consulting with her. She felt almost like a piece of furniture they were all terribly fond of, or had come to depend upon, or whatever it was they individually thought about her — but she didn't feel like a total entity, a human being with wishes and desires and a mind of her own.

However, she'd been around enough monied people to have learned that they frequently had such an attitude. It was not in the least unusual for the affluent to take others for granted. And Jeannine couldn't help feeling somewhat hurt by their insensibility; she had come to expect more from the de Lorcas. Why, she wasn't sure — but she had. She had to remind herself, even while they were speaking, that she was nothing more than a paid employee, and that she had presumed too much. They had not let her down; she had expected more than was her right.

Finally, Miguel rose and kissed his grandmother on the forehead. "All right, Doña Josefina, have it your own way. I do *not* agree with you nor do I approve, but if you want to keep the police out of this for a while longer, so be it." He crossed over to the sideboard and returned his glass to the tray with a furrowed brow and an expression of reluctant acquiescence, then scanned the room as if it were the last time he'd ever see it. His eyes dark and troubled, met Jeannine's. His smile was unexpected, and though warm and sincere, it seemed to contain hundreds of secrets that she would never know. "And you, Jeannine? What would you like to do under the circumstances? This cannot be very pleasant for you . . . in fact, as you already know, it could be quite dangerous."

She could barely hold back tears of grateful relief. Someone did care, after all! She was not the de Lorca chattel, and her emotional gratitude was out of proportion to the kindness. "I-I'm willing to accept the majority vote. Whatever y-you think is best is fine." Now that her opinion had been requested, she was perfectly willing to put her life in their hands, to join the dogs in a twenty-four-hour vigilance if necessary.

"You're not afraid to be here without us?" Miguel asked softly.

Jeannine shook her head; even if she were, nothing could have forced her to admit it at that point. "I couldn't leave Doña Josefina here all alone. . . ."

La señora smiled her approval. "The girl is not a quitter, Miguel. I could tell that from her handwriting!"

It was, Jeannine thought, a rather strange thing to say at that moment; but then, she remembered that she had had to submit her application to Mrs. de Lorca in her own handwriting. And it suddenly occurred to Jeannine that the woman had used handwriting analysis to replace a personal interview. What an incredible woman she was!

"Well, I've got to stop by the office," Miguel said, picking up his jacket and heading toward the foyer.

"Will you be home for dinner?" la señora wanted to know.

"I don't know yet," he replied. "I'll telephone you later and let you know."

La señora walked to the door with him,

then excused herself to go upstairs for a nap. The tension and excitement had exhausted her. Jeannine accompanied her to be sure she was all right and comfortable, and when she returned to the living room, John was standing, pouring himself another drink. "John! Your shoulder! You shouldn't be walking around yet. . . ."

"Oh, it's fine. Besides, I'm pouring with my other hand. Want some?"

She declined and went to sit down on the deep cushioned divan facing the balcony and its superb view. Briefly, she lapsed into a consideration of her decision to stay on. What would Vincent Sternig, M.D., have to say about her decision? He would doubtlessly bawl her out as an overly loyal fool . . . but she was confident that he would understand. Jeannine suddenly felt too much like a member of the family to just walk out on them now.

Her thoughts had strayed so far that she was unaware of John's presence next to her on the divan. Or, more accurately, she was only peripherally aware; her attention was elsewhere. Consequently, she was totally unprepared when John took her chin with his hand, turned her face toward him, then leaned forward and kissed her softly on the lips.

"Are you worried?" he asked, amusement in his eyes.

For an instant, she was unsure about the nature of his question; worried about the situation in general, or worried about his kiss. It had been such a discreet kiss that she decided upon the former. "No. Not really. Concerned, yes."

John pulled her closer and rested her head upon his good shoulder. "I'll have to be leaving soon, Jeannie. I'm not going to like being away from you."

"I'll miss you," she said sincerely.

"Will you? Will you miss me? How much?"

Before she could reply, he'd leaned forward and took her mouth with his, hungrily, almost roughly, while his hand took hold of her long red hair and held her head rigidly where he wanted it. John's breath became ragged with his prolonged kiss, and when his lips left hers, they traveled to her neck. His hand moved to her arm and his fingers dug into her flesh. He was being too rough, and too unexpectedly aggressive; it was unnerving her. She could feel beads of perspiration on John's forehead, and she knew that his physical need for her would not be easily dissuaded if she didn't put a stop to his lovemaking soon.

"Don't, John. Now now. . . ."

"Why not? I've wasted too much time as it is," he breathed against her flesh. Nonetheless, he did loosen his hold upon her and she was able to move away from him somewhat.

John stared at her for a moment, scrutinizing her, then leaned forward and took a long swallow from his drink. "I'm surprised at you, Jeannie. I hadn't taken you for a tease."

She looked at him incredulously.

"Well, what would you call it? You don't think I've been hanging around just for the pleasure of Miguel's sour company, do you?"

Jeannine could hardly believe her ears. Had he had too much to drink? Or had he thought she was some sort of common trollop on his grandmother's payroll? She made a move to stand up, to leave the room, but John's hand restrained her.

"Look, I'm not asking anything out of the ordinary of you. You're an attractive young woman, and I'm a normal male. What else did you expect after all the time we've spent together?"

"I think you'd better let me go, John," she said tersely. His remarks were too cynical, too hard, for her to handle comfortably.

She had never been in this sort of situation before, and she wished with all her might it was not happening at all.

"I suppose you're the type who wants a promise of marriage first?" He grinned as if nothing could be funnier.

Jeannine was absolutely baffled by John's sudden personality change. Gone was the affable, charming young man; in his place was a calloused, crude, and offensive Mr. Hyde. "Are you drunk?" she asked in a flat tone.

"Me? You've got to be joking!"

"Then what's come over you, John?"

He stood up and went to stand before one of the paintings as if appraising its merits or worth. Finally, without turning around to look at her, he said, "Perhaps I find myself caring a little too much about you . . . perhaps I just wanted to find out what kind of a girl you really are."

His voice seemed distant, a factual monotone. Jeannine was thoroughly confused and wanted desperately to leave, to go to her room and think things through. She rose and silently crossed the room to the door, where she paused long enough to say, "I hope you have your answer now."

John did not turn around as she left the living room, and by the time she was halfway up the stairs, she could feel the tears spilling over and running down her cheeks. It had been a humiliating and frightening experience — whatever had possessed him! Yet even as she mounted the stairs, Jeannine found herself in need of someone to confide in; trying to sort out the complicated personalities and problems of the de Lorca family definitely required another head. Her tears ceased as abruptly as they had begun, and she whirled on her heels and ran back down the stairs, through the doorway, and to the small VW.

The car's noisy engine turned over instantly, and within seconds she was driving down the winding road, past the huge fir, and toward the village of Carmel. She didn't know where Aaron Franklin lived . . . but someone in town would be able to tell her.

Chapter 12

The doctor did not even seem surprised when she knocked at the front door of his modest cottage on Pescadero Drive. Her mood also didn't seem to shock him. It was already night by the time she arrived, and Aaron Franklin admitted her as if she were expected, handing her a mug of hot cider with a cinnamon stick in it.

"I rather thought you might come here," he said warmly. He stood at the fireplace stoking the kindling in an effort to get the fire going properly and ward off the chill of the room.

Jeannine cupped her hands around the mug, drawing warmth from it. Now that she was there, she found herself rather uncertain of what to say. "I suppose you know about the sniper?"

Dr. Franklin sat down opposite her. "Yes. Everyone knows about it by now. Have they caught the fellow yet?"

"No. They're not likely to either. Mrs. de Lorca doesn't want to call in the police."

He arched his eyebrows above tolerantly

amused eyes. "Well, naturally, the police know about it too. But then, there's nothing they can officially do about it unless a report is filed."

"She's afraid of the publicity . . . she said."

Dr. Franklin propped his feet up on the battered round table that stood between them, resting the heels of his scuffed shoes on a stack of magazines which must have been more than a year old. "And you don't think that's the real reason."

"No." Jeannine felt terribly disloyal confiding this to the one man la señora had asked her to avoid; but there was no one else she could turn to. "I need your help, Dr. Franklin. I'm confused, and I think I might even be a bit scared. . . ."

His kindly eyes crinkled at the corners. "As well you should be."

"Just what *is* going on at 'Puerta de Paz'? I'm so confused I'm becoming paranoid! Why would anyone want to cause any harm to the de Lorcas . . . and why do you and Mrs. de Lorca avoid each other? I know I'm being terribly impertinent, asking questions about things that shouldn't be any of my business, but. . . ."

"Not at all! On the contrary, Jeannine, it *is* your business. What if that sniper's shot had hit you instead of John? You're very much involved, and you've every right to know."

His attitude filled Jeannine with an enormous sense of relief. For once someone was not treating her like an innocent teenager who had to be shielded from the ugly facts of life. For the first time since coming to Carmel-by-the-Sea, she was being treated as a responsible adult. Recognizing that the doctor was not going to fill her up with stalls and gibberish, with evasiveness, she could feel much of her tension leaving her. She blew on the steaming mug of cider, and sipped the scalding liquid like a child settling in to hear a good, long story.

"First of all, you must realize that there is more to all of this than you've been told. Josefina is not merely interested in conservation; she's not quite the altruistic matriarch she's made out to be by those on her committees. Much of the Carmel Valley she's striving so hard to keep out of the hands of industry or land developers is *her own* property! Under the terms of the Spanish land grants, Ignacio de Lorca owned a considerable number of acres throughout this area. He was an incredibly wealthy man and not a totally scrupulous one. Ignacio grew up in Mexico, and there he learned of his claim to lands up here under the old Spanish laws. After years of litigation, he managed to regain control of the lands. But after all those years, many people had built their homes there — humble as they might be — and they tilled the soil, and to all intents and purposes, believed it to be theirs. Ignacio threw them out and converted the land to grazing grounds for his cattle."

Jeannine was fascinated and listened avidly. "That wouldn't make him a very popular man, would it?" she remarked casually.

"Perhaps you didn't know that Ignacio de Lorca was murdered not long thereafter. Josefina, at the time, had only been married to him for about five years . . . and she adored Ignacio completely. Josefina had been married off — a family-arranged matter — at the age of fifteen to a man infinitely older than she, too old to give her children.

"She tried to bury her maternal instincts in good works around the community, and often would help the Sisters at the nearby convent to take care of their orphaned children. But nothing could quite replace her sense of barren emptiness, no matter how hard she tried to adjust. Finally, though, her husband grew ill and died. Josefina, then in her early thirties, was a widow.

"I'm giving you approximate ages only because there were no records kept in those days. More cider?" he asked, pausing in his monologue.

Jeannine extended her cup to him and watched the man's steady hand holding the heavy teapot in which he kept the brew warm above the fire. "How did you learn all this about her?"

Aaron Franklin smiled and returned to his seat. "Gossip, mostly, and what bits and pieces Josefina herself has let drop over the years. But I've been able to piece much of it together and weed out what seemed unlikely or impossible."

"Go on, please," she urged.

"Well, she met Ignacio de Lorca about two years later. He was dashing and proud, somewhat younger than she, and he was *macho*, through and through. The sun rose and fell on Ignacio de Lorca as far as Josefina was concerned. And her joy was boundless when she became pregnant by him. Josefina and Ignacio had two children; one died of diphtheria around the age of nine, but the other one, a son, survived. He in turn had two children who ultimately became the parents, respectively, of Olga and John, and of Miguel."

Jeannine remarked that la señora must

have been very much in love with Ignacio.

"Yes, I suppose she was. So you can imagine her reaction when Ignacio was murdered. Josefina went into a mourning that rivaled Queen Victoria's! She was inconsolable. Even her children seemed of little or no comfort to her."

"So she substituted his lands for his arms," Jeannine guessed.

"With a compulsive vengeance!" Dr. Franklin affirmed. "Her every waking moment is spent protecting and preserving Ignacio's lands. The Carmel Valley is growing, Jeannine, whether she likes it or not. I've seen some of the plans submitted to her of proposed shopping centers, or apartment buildings — all of them, with rare exception, have been done with the utmost care to keep the country flavor of the area, to avoid crowding and congestion. No one has suggested that she sell *all* of her land, only those portions that are near the highway and would lend themselves to improving the area."

"But isn't that what everyone says at first, and then when it's too late you find out that the project backers are crooks? If you give an acre now, isn't it just a matter of a few years before the entire area is just another suburb?"

"Not necessarily, but that's not the issue right now. What is the point is her obsessiveness about it. You can always find ways of controlling progress, but to think you can stop it is a very colonial attitude."

"All right, so she's made many enemies. Do you think one of them is causing all the trouble? Is it some kind of conspiracy to frighten her into selling land? That doesn't seem very logical."

"Perhaps not logical — but feasible. I don't pretend to know who's behind all this. Maybe no one is. Maybe it's just coincidence."

"La señora rather prefers that theory herself," Jeannine said with a light laugh. "But then, tell me, what is her feud with you? What is this terrible cloak of secrecy whenever your name is mentioned?"

Dr. Franklin sat forward placing his mug carefully at the edge of the table. His face betrayed the indecision within him, as if he wanted to tell Jeannine but was not yet certain that she could be trusted with the truth. "I wish I could tell you — I want you to believe that."

Jeannine's disappointment was tremendous but she could not even bring herself to argue with him, to protest her reliability.

"I'm sorry, Jeannine. The feud between us

is very, very personal. It could alter too many lives for me to risk telling anyone, even you. I am sorry, my dear, — I genuinely am."

Jeannine nearly collided with Miguel turning off Highway 1 on her return to the hacienda. Her frustration had converted to fury, and though she knew better, she was driving the small Volkswagen with a chip on her shoulder, as if daring all other cars on the road to see what would happen if they didn't get out of her way. Miguel had swerved sufficiently to avert collision, honking at her to pull over once the turn was completed. But in Jeannine's state of mind, she not only didn't pay any attention, she didn't even realize who was honking at her.

Her smaller vehicle tore up the winding curves much faster than Miguel's car could, and she came to a crunching, squealing stop just before the open garage door. Fists clenched, a burning flush in her cheeks, she stormed the front door and strode into the living room with all the purposefulness of a Wagnerian heroine. Unfortunately, no one was in there to see the expression on her face, or the way she flung her body and slouched into the divan's cushions. Arms akimbo, she sat like a boulder staring out the windows blankly. She was only dimly aware of another car pulling onto the graveled driveway, or of the front door's opening and closing. Even the barking of the dogs failed to attract her attention; probably because she'd become so accustomed to their chronic announcement of arrivals and departures.

"Well, now, just what has gotten into you, young lady!" Miguel demanded as he entered the room. "Somebody tie a tincan to your tail?"

Jeannine glanced up at him through hazel eyes turned battleship gray with futile rage, her mouth set in a grim, tight line. It didn't help that Miguel seemed to be slightly amused by her behavior.

"How about a drink . . . that might ease some of that fury." He fixed them both martinis and came to sit down near to her, where John had sat earlier in the day. "Want to talk to me about it?" he asked softly.

"How *can* I," she answered with a quivering voice, "when no one, but *no* one, will tell me what's *really* going on around here!" She took too large a sip from her drink and sputtered mildly.

"All right, all right," Miguel said, laughing good-naturedly, "take it easy. Tell me what's bothering you, and I'll try to help.

But you've got to tell me calmly, without histrionics."

Jeannine took a deep breath and let it out slowly. She glanced at Miguel's rugged dark face and wondered if he truly would be honest with her. His expression was one of amusement, yes, but there was also sincere concern in his eyes. She took a discreet sip of her martini, then leaned back and forcibly tried to relax. After a few moments of collecting herself, she related to Miguel, as calmly as she could, the things that had been bothering her, and her fruitless visit to Dr. Franklin — and why she had gone to him. Prudently, she made no mention of John's erratic behavior early in the day. When she'd told Miguel everything, a heavy sigh escaped her. "I suppose you're going to tell me it's none of my business, or that there are some things I am not supposed to know. . . ."

Miguel had listened attentively, without interruption, but now he was no longer amused. "In a sense, you're right on both counts." He rose and crossed over to the windows before the balcony, his hands deep in his pockets, his back a muscled wall to her eyes. "I would be lying if I said that it didn't matter that you went to see Aaron Franklin. If Doña Josefina finds out,

155

she will be very, very upset."

"But you, personally, don't think there was any harm in it?"

"No. I don't see why there should be — other than the fact that Aaron's a well-known town gossip when he chooses to be. At other times, he is the pillar of discretion. Let's hope he truly likes you enough to keep your confidence intact. I'm pleased to know that he kept the source of the feud private . . . that, Jeannine, truly is none of your business."

"Oh, good grief!" Jeannine sighed.

"But I can tell you this much . . . it involves my great-grandmother's will, which in turn means that it involves John, Olga, and me. The terms of Doña Josefina's will are unknown to anyone except her lawyers in San Francisco. No, I didn't draw up the will; it would have been unethical to do so. I don't know if I'm inheriting the technically legal one dollar or one thousand dollars to be sure I cannot contest the will, or if it contains a three-way division of all of Doña Josefina's material fortune. None of us know. Obviously, it shouldn't be too much longer before we all find out; la señora cannot go on very much longer."

"But what does Dr. Franklin have to do with la señora's will? That should be none of his business. . . ."

Miguel smiled. "Pot calling the kettle black?"

Jeannine could not deny the allegation and returned his smile sheepishly. "Well, his life's not being threatened because someone's after one of you."

"Granted. Which is why I'm willing to tell you as much as I can — you deserve some kind of explanation, Jeannine, but there are some things I shall not be able to tell you. Not yet, anyway."

"That reminds me," she interrupted. "Why did you say what you did that first morning we had breakfast together . . . about wondering if I'd come to the right place or not."

Miguel shrugged. "I had reason to suspect that there might be trouble brewing around here. You know, of course, about the proposed dam site, inland on the Carmel Valley Road?"

Jeannine nodded. She'd typed quite a few of Mrs. de Lorca's letters to the chairman of that project, and had overheard the woman on the telephone to various committee members who wished to prevent the dam from being built.

"Then you also know that the entire matter is going up for vote on a special ballot next month. The building of this dam is for a private water supply to be sold to local ranchers. It's not a public utility for the benefit of the entire region."

"Yes, yes," Jeannine said rather impatiently.

"Grandmother has almost single-handedly blocked that company getting its approval from anyone. In a maneuver of desperation — they have, after all, spent hundreds of thousands of dollars on it already — they managed to get the whole project on a special ballot for public vote. Needless to say, they're relying on voter apathy; if the local residents don't bother to vote, then their own interested investors will put it through by default."

"So why should they bother to threaten either of you?"

"Because they cannot be certain of their success! Life would be much simpler for them if Doña Josefina were out of the way."

"But," Jeannine persisted, "even if she were out of the way, it she passed on, there would still be you or John or Olga to contend with."

"Ah, there's the problem, you see." Miguel refreshed their drinks and came back to sit beside her. "That's why the contents of her will is a subject of such vital interest to these people. If John or Olga or both of them were to receive control of the lands, or the bulk of the estate, or what have you, anybody could buy their approval. Even if it's divided into equal thirds, they would have the majority vote."

"But if you get the bulk of the estate . . . ?"

Miguel shrugged as if the question were irrelevant. "Then, they know they're in deep trouble. I am in complete accord with la señora on this issue — though we have often argued about others. As the population increases, one must provide more water, more electricity, even more roads. But this is not for the public, it is for the benefit of private enterprise to get richer, and in the doing, to deface our valley."

"Then it would certainly seem that, somehow, in some way, Dr. Franklin knows the terms of la señora's will!" Jeannine exclaimed excitedly, the pieces beginning to fit together.

"It's not likely," Miguel drawled slowly, "but it is possible. Though how he could manage such a thing, I'll never fathom."

"Does he stand to profit in some way if this project goes through?"

"Not that I know of. As you've seen for yourself, he is not a man given to material possessions. I've never known him to display any form of greed."

They both fell silent for a few moments, each engaged in his own private speculation. "Then," Jeannine said, breaking the stillness, "you think these accidents may have been arranged by the proponents of the dam?"

"It would make the most sense . . . unless Doña Josefina should happen to be correct with her coincidence theory. It wouldn't matter very much who got hurt so long as it served to scare off Grandmother. And, of course, if she herself were the victim, so much the better."

"Then why won't she call in the police!"

Miguel ran his strong fingers through his dark curly hair, an expression of exasperation on his face. "You heard her! She doesn't want to lose her supporters in this fight, and she's afraid that it would look like a vulgar publicity stunt to discredit the proponents of the dam project. And she's probably right! It could look like that."

"Oh, sure! John would shoot himself in the shoulder, and drive himself off the road!"

"Now that you mention it, it would certainly seem as if it's one of John's enemies more than our grandmother's. He's been friends with a few gangsters over the years, and he is a heavy gambler as well. That is another possibility. Which is the hell of this matter! We just don't have enough to go on!"

"Well," Jeannine said, exhaling heavily, "I suppose I know a little more than I did before . . . but not much. I do want to thank you, Miguel. At least you've tried to take some of the worry off my shoulders . . . that was very kind of you."

He rested his hand on her head, his fingers toying lightly with the thick strands of red hair, and then stood up abruptly. "In that case," he said, back to his former austere facade, "we'd both better go upstairs and get ready for dinner. We don't want to keep *abuelita* waiting!"

Jeannine smiled feebly and watched him leave the room. What a strange man he was! So ferocious one moment, and so tender and sweet the next. . . .

Chapter 13

Shortly after coffee, there was a resounding playful knock at the huge front door. La señora glanced up with an exasperated expression of "Who dares to intrude uninvited" but nodded to Manuel to answer. He could be heard making his way down the hall, his leather heels clicking for a few steps on the tiles, then muted as he crossed the oriental throwrugs, then clicking again; and with his progress, the clicking of Hans's nails right behind him like maracas and castanets. The brute animal was snarling as the two of them approached the door, and began to bark in earnest when Manuel opened it.

Manuel entered the dining room moments later. "It's señorita Olga," he said with a perplexed expression on his face.

"Then why isn't she with you?" la señora wanted to know.

"She say she is afraid to come in while the dog is loose," Manuel replied.

"Oh, for pity's sake," Miguel muttered and rose to his feet.

Jeannine could not resist smiling to herself; she could easily visualize helpless Olga standing at the threshold, arms folded, stubbornly refusing to walk past Hans — fortunately, Olga didn't know about Bruno yet, who was barking in the kitchen behind the closed door.

In seconds, Miguel had quieted Hans, and Olga's voice ripped shrilly through the foyer. "Well, really, Miguel, when a person can't even come to her own family home without some vicious beast leaping at her . . ."

And Miguel's stern rebuff, "He did no such thing, Olga. We have the dogs here for a very, very good reason!"

"Dogs? More than this one? Spare me!"

As Miguel led Hans off toward the kitchen, Olga entered the dining room, breathless and flushed. She immediately crossed over to her great-grandmother and gave her a dutiful peck on the cheek, then glanced over to Jeannine and winked at her conspiratorially. "I suppose John got shot in a duel over you?"

"How'd you know I was shot?" John wanted to know immediately, his indignation obvious.

"Silly," she teased, walking around the table and sitting down at Miguel's chair. "Just

163

about everyone in San Francisco knows you've been shot! They're all just buzzing with curiosity, and I decided that the only proper sisterly thing to do would be to drive down and comfort you."

"I'd no idea you were so famous," Miguel said, reentering the room and lifting another chair to the table. He poured coffee for them all, but his aggravation was apparent.

"Now you *know* that John and I have many, many friends," Olga said. "It was just bound to get around once somebody got wind of it."

"And how," la señora interrupted, "did the wind reach San Francisco?"

"I don't know," Olga answered, leaning forward and inspecting the dessert plates still on the table. "Is there any more of that? I'm *famished!*"

"Probably some local reporter trying to drum up a story for himself," John said.

La señora summoned Chata with the crystal table-bell and instructed her to bring Olga a sandwich and some dessert. "Nonetheless, Olga, it was very good of you to come down to see your brother. As you can tell for yourself, he is doing quite nicely."

"Yes, I see, but *how* did it *happen!*" Olga asked, her curiosity obviously outweighing her concern.

After all that had been happening around "Puerta de Paz," Jeannine was delighted to see the irrepressible Olga. It was like opening a window on a smoke-filled room.

"It was an accident," Miguel said forcefully, leaving John no room to argue the point.

"That's all?" Olga asked, obviously disappointed.

"That's all."

"Oh, dear. Well, that's not what I'd call something to tell KCBS for the evening news!"

"Hopefully, Olga, nothing that happens here would ever qualify for such notoriety," la señora said, nearly harrumphing.

There was a rather strained silence for a few awkward moments, and finally Miguel rose from his chair. "Sorry to have to leave," he said, "but I've got a case in court tomorrow and I have to go over my brief."

"Really?" Olga chirped. "A *murder* case?"

"No," he replied rather tersely. "A migrant worker lost his leg when a tractor overturned. I've filed a negligence suit for him."

"Oh," Olga said, quickly losing interest in the entire matter.

Miguel crossed to his grandmother and kissed her hand in deferential departure,

165

waved to John, and merely nodded to Jeannine.

Jeannine tried to turn the conversation onto something lighter. "It's really wonderful to see you again, Olga," she said. "Will you be staying long? I promised to show you where I bought that kaftan, remember?"

Olga had wolfed down her sandwich and was already busy at work on her dessert. "No, luv, I can't stay long. I've just *got* to be back tomorrow afternoon. I've the most *wonderful* date tomorrow night . . . oh, he's gorgeous! You'd love him!"

"I rather doubt that," John threw in.

"Tell you what, though," Olga said, ignoring his comment. "Why don't we take a run into the Village in the morning and then we could perhaps lunch together. That would be *fun!* I don't know how you *stand* it around here otherwise! Nothing to do, nowhere to go. Brrr!"

"Don't you want to know how I got shot anymore?" John asked petulantly.

"Of *course* I do, darling, of course!"

La señora and Jeannine worked the following morning until around eleven-thirty; trying to get anything done while Olga was in the house was virtually impossible. Her voice seemed to carry into every room like spring air through schoolroom windows, and her gay laughter was as welcome as the dismissal bell. While Olga might not have been the most intellectual or altruistic person in the world, at that moment in time she was the best possible tonic for Jeannine.

Finally la señora threw down her pen in fatalistic resignation to the latest peal of laughter from John and Olga. Jeannine impetuously gave the woman a hug before she ran to get her scarf and a light jacket. She found the two of them in the living room, Olga regaling John with tales of their mutual friends: who had behaved monstrously at a party, who was going with whom, and all the usual trivia Jeannine would have attributed to teenagers rather than adults.

"There you are!" Olga exclaimed as she spotted Jeannine entering the room. "Thought you'd *never* stop that awful typing!"

Jeannine smiled. She couldn't have explained why, but Olga made her feel like a sophomore in college at an endless pajama party. The drastic change from the recent dismal surroundings and long faces was like walking from a funeral into the midst of a gypsy wedding. "I'm ready whenever you are," she said, her bright-green floral scarf hanging limply from her hand.

"Off we are," Olga gaily replied.

"Hold on!" John interrupted. "Where are you two going?"

"Out."

"Why can't I go too?"

"Because," Olga said, trying to imitate la señora's deep voice, "we have much to discuss and wish to enjoy our privacy."

They left the room with John sputtering, and crossed the gravel driveway to the garage where Olga had parked her Porsche. In no time, they were down the mountainside and looking for a parking space in downtown Carmel, near the Butcher Shop, where they planned to rip into a nice, juicy prime rib. Olga had already explained that she didn't want to try on any clothes until after lunch, that she wanted to be sure whatever she bought would be comfortable no matter how much she gorged herself.

Afterwards, they stopped at the little dress shop Jeannine had discovered, browsed a bit, and finding nothing they really liked, they decided to take the Seventeen-Mile Drive. They entered from the Village and Olga seemed to sober almost at once, as if the National Park had some sort of magic hold upon her. As they drove in silence past the pine and cypress, the expanse of cerulean ocean beyond them dotted with boulders and reefs, Jeannine could feel the change come over Olga; she was suddenly thoughtful, serious, and perhaps even somewhat apprehensive.

"Was John's accident really that simple?" Olga asked softly.

Jeannine, while noticing the shift in Olga's mood, was not prepared for that particular question. "Surely he told you all about it," she hedged.

Olga took her eyes off the narrow, winding road for only a moment, long enough to peer at Jeannine. "He told me *his* version. Someone must've been cleaning a rifle and it went off accidentally or something silly like that."

"But you don't believe him?"

"Well, good grief! Monster killer dogs running all over the place, doom and gloom written on all your faces! I can't remember *when* I've seen Grandmother look so drawn, so tense. Look, Jeannie, everyone seems to think I've the brains of a gnat simply because I don't like to get all involved in things, all uptight about the state of the world or politics. I simply don't wish to know about such things. If they are bad news, let them be bad news without my help. I want fun from my life, not a broken back from shouldering the burdens of the world!"

Jeannine had heard similar arguments from many people she had encountered in her previous work; people who shut out the rest of the world, people who were unable to face any responsibility beyond their "own backyards." She was fully able to understand such an attitude; yet compared to people like señora de Lorca and her love for the Carmel Valley, or even Miguel's championing of the Chicano community, it seemed shallow and empty as a way of life.

"I suppose you think I'm just a selfish, spoiled brat," Olga prompted, a child's smile on her lips very similar to John's grin when he knew he was being foolish.

"That's a loaded question," Jeannine parried.

"Well, don't let the noble spirits of this world kid you. La señora may have her conservation cause, but does she *know* what's going on in the Mideast . . . will her conservation attempts stop another war? We all have our especial interests to champion . . . I'm just more honest than most people. My especial interest is *me*. Because John is my brother, he's included — more or less. And if someone's taking potshots at him, I want to know about it."

"I can appreciate that," Jeannine said softly. "And I only wish I could tell you what's going on . . . but frankly, Olga, I don't know either. It has to do with some dam project, with Mrs. de Lorca's interference, and I suppose, to some degree, from what little I've been able to gather, with the terms of la señora's will."

"Oh God! *That* again!"

"Again?" Jeannine asked, but her attention was somewhat distracted as they rounded a curve and came upon the famous Ghost Tree, a gnarled cypress that looked as if it had been sculpted, with lush straight pines surrounding it, accenting its peculiar shape.

"Oh, John's always rapping on and on about her will, who's going to inherit the whole schmeer and all that."

"Don't you care?" Jeannine said lightly, somewhat amused by Olga's attitude.

"Not really. Logic says she has to divide it all up equally among the three of us. But presuming she didn't . . . so what? If John gets the bulk of it, he'll take very good care of me . . . and if Miguel gets it, he would too — although I've no doubt I'd have to struggle for every penny."

Jeannine considered her rather philosophical attitude toward such a vast inheritance, and silently agreed it was not only the path of least resistance, but a very logical approach. "Of course, you could be the one who gets it all, couldn't you?"

Olga slammed her hand against the steering wheel, laughing heartily. "Not bloody likely! We're a *latin* family, Jeannie. Girls don't rank very high. Besides, *bisabuelita* knows perfectly well I'd squander it all; she'd be absolutely right to have someone else take care of my interests."

"You really aren't worried, are you?" she said, somewhat in awe of such trust. Jeannine was not at all sure that she would have such an accepting attitude under similar circumstances. Perhaps, she thought to herself, I'm not such a naive goose after all.

Olga shrugged her reply, then became serious again. "It's out of my hands. I've known that all my life. One or both of the boys will dole out my allowance, and that's that. I'm no scrapper. Even if I had some legal recourse, I wouldn't *bother* with such things. Let's face it, Jeannie, I'm irresponsible and a spendthrift — I don't blame our great-grandmother for having more sense than I do."

Not knowing what would be the polite thing to say after such an admission, Jeannine remained silent. They drove on through the winding curves at a very slow speed, each apparently quietly introspective. Past Point Lobos with its jutting rocks where the rushing surf broke up into a thundering explosion of foam and spray; beyond the twisted and dead cypresses, their bleached branches like tendrils of doom covered with blood-red algae. The entire area was almost too beautiful to be believed; alternately peaceful and violent, spectacular and pastoral. Jeannine could not help but find an analogy between the scenic drive and what had been happening at "Puerta de Paz." The glaring difference, of course, was that the violence at the hacienda was manmade and someone would be a deliberate victim of it all.

She glanced discreetly at Olga and once again wondered how she could have such an insular view of her life and her world. She obviously truly did not care what was happening so long as she received enough money to continue in her present lifestyle. Jeannine questioned if Olga were truly as happy and carefree as she seemed; if in the quiet of the night when sleep was denied her, did she not then have doubts and fears, did she not question the lack of meaning to her existence? As alien as it was to Jeannine's own character, she rather assumed that Olga spent no sleepless nights, and that it never occurred to her to question anything beyond what she was going to wear to the next ball.

Olga returned to San Francisco that afternoon, and the evening seemed to drag on forever. The conversation at dinner was strained, as if they were acting out parts in a play none of them had read. There was no significant reason for it, that Jeannine could account for; unless, perhaps, they were all feeling the letdown of Olga's departure. Jeannine realized that she probably wasn't the only one who had enjoyed Olga's visit as a respite from the threatening events of the past few weeks.

In Jeannine's mind, however, the lack of Olga's capricious personality at the table seemed to plunge them back into even deeper contemplation. Worse, Jeannine was finding it quite difficult to be at the same table with John after his crude advance the day before. Somehow, Olga had acted as a temporary buffer, virtually eradicating those unpleasant moments with John.

And John seemed to sense it as well. He averted his eyes from Jeannine, she was happy to note; at least he had the decency to be ashamed of himself!

Quietly, they partook of their evening meal. Each time Chata entered the dining room with a new course, Bruno followed her as if he were her own personal bodyguard; Hans, on the other hand, could be seen through the swinging door, dozing beneath the kitchen table with his massive head resting on Manuel's boot. Manuel seemed accustomed to the dog's devotion, and ate his dinner contentedly with a folded copy of *La Prensa* before him. Jeannine could not get over how quickly the dogs had become family members — but she could not quite forget that they were trained killers, as well.

After dinner, they retired to the living room for coffee and brandy, but the atmosphere was so awkward that Jeannine excused herself early. She closed the door to her room softly, then flipped on an FM station for some quiet, classical music while she drew her bath. Ordinarily, Jeannine preferred showers; but the tension of the past few weeks called for a long, luxurious hot bath. When the tub was full, she sampled the water's temperature with one foot; it was uncomfortably hot, but she was determined. Gradually, she sank her entire body into the water, wincing slightly, and let her torso slip forward until she was neck-deep in bath oil and bubbles, her arms floating to the surface as she relaxed more and more.

When she'd completed her ablutions, Jeannine propped herself up in bed and resumed reading a book on the history of the Monterey Peninsula. From time to time, sounds from the kitchen would drift up to her room through the open windows; apparently, Manuel had brought the portable TV into the kitchen while he worked at something else. He was very fond of watching the Mexican variety shows on Channel 34, and he frequently had the set on if he thought he'd have an hour or more free.

Everything seemed so normal and peaceful, it was difficult for Jeannine to accept any of the recent events at "Puerta de Paz." Her mind strayed from her reading as she tried to envision some blackguard entrepreneur, complete with mustache and top hat and cape, threatening the premises for his own evil gain. No one did things like that anymore, she was sure; tying the heroine to the railroad tracks was passé.

But if not the proponents of the dam project — who else? Who would go to so much trouble, and for what? It just didn't make sense otherwise. Her busy imagination had toyed briefly, that afternoon, with the idea that perhaps Dr. Franklin might be involved; but to what purpose, if he had nothing to gain? Even if he had, somehow, learned the contents of Doña Josefina's will, it couldn't possibly matter to him other than as advance gossip.

John, of course, seemed the most likely of them all as a target — but he was too casual about it all, too disinterested. Surely he would be the first one to suspect if his own life were in danger.

These speculations spiraled in Jeannine's mind until she fell fast asleep, the book in her lap, and the nightstand lamp still glowing. In very short order, her breathing became deeper and slower, all tensions slipping from her body quietly.

She awoke in terror, gasping for air beneath the pillow that covered her face. Jeannine grabbed wildly, trying to get it away from her nose, and realized with horror and panic that a man's arms were holding the pillow in place. She couldn't see, of course, and her mind operated on the survival instinct rather than logical planning. Thrashing frantically, she wrestled and tugged at the arms, feeling the fine hairs about the wrists; her heart pounding wildly as she tried to free herself.

In the struggle, she had pushed the bed linens to the floor and once her legs were unencumbered, she kicked out violently at her assailant. She dimly heard a muffled cry as one foot connected with his thigh, and felt one hand try to capture her ankles. Whoever he was, he had just lost the advantage. There was no way for him to keep her face covered with the pillow with just one hand, while she wriggled and kicked at him. As if sensing his weakened position, knowing it was only a matter of time before she was able to break away from him, he let go of her and the pillow simultaneously, then bolted for her bedroom window.

Jeannine heard his exit through the window even as she sat upright and screamed for all she was worth, gasping for air at the same time, and shaking with fear.

Within moments, Miguel and John came bounding up the stairs and, without bothering to knock, ran into her room. John spotted the open window first and went toward it immediately. Miguel, on the other hand, gave his immediate attention to Jeannine. He strode to her bedside and took Jeannine in his arms, rocking her, holding her, comforting her.

"What happened, Jeannine? A nightmare?" He held her closely, his hand on her head as if cradling a child. "Shh, shh," he whispered, "it's all right now."

"Not a sign of anyone," John said. "Probably just a bad dream."

"Turn on the light," Miguel said to his cousin. "It will make her feel more secure."

John crossed to the door and flipped on the switch. Both men then took a long look at Jeannine's face, at the panic that was etched in her eyes. Her sobs had diminished and she was in much better control of herself when la señora, with Manuel's help, entered the room. *"Bueno, bueno, pero qué conmoción,"* she said.

Miguel stood up and went to look out the window for himself.

"S-someone t-tried to kill me," Jeannine managed to say at last. "I s-still d-don't quite have my breath back."

Miguel spun on his heels and stared directly into Jeannine's eyes. "What!"

Doña Josefina sat down on the edge of the bed and took Jeannine's hand in her own. "What are you saying, *niña?*"

The girl nodded, already feeling the stiffness of so much physical exertion. "It's true," she said softly.

It was then that la señora seemed to notice the rapidly appearing bruises on Jeannine's arms where her attacker had tried to subdue her. "Did you see who it was?" la señora asked in a very calm, matter-of-fact manner.

"No," Jeannine answered. "I awoke with a pillow over my face, gasping for air. I saw nothing."

"My God!" John exclaimed. "This has gone too far!" He placed his hand over his bandaged shoulder as if for emphasis.

"Oh, shut up, John," Miguel said, not unkindly. "And what happened when he let go of you, when he ran out the window?"

Jeannine shrugged, suddenly terribly conscious of the fact that she was in her nightgown, her soft white shoulders and throat exposed, and more of her bosom showing than would have been considered proper; apparently her gown had torn during the struggle. She was acutely aware of Miguel's uneasiness, of the way he tried to look only into her eyes — but couldn't seem to keep his gaze from returning to her throat.

"No," she answered at last. "It was too dark, for one thing. For another, I was already hysterical with fear. I wouldn't have recognized my own mother in the first few seconds following what happened." She attempted a smile, then said, "Ever had anyone try to asphyxiate you?"

La señora gestured to Manuel to get Jeannine's robe from the chair in the corner, then placed it over the girl's shoulders. She then leaned forward and took one of Jeannine's pills from the nightstand and handed it to her with a glass of water. "Here, before you have another attack."

Jeannine accepted the glass with shaking hands, her whole body shivering from the horror of what had transpired. She swallowed her pill, then gratefully handed the glass back to la señora. "You know," she said thoughtfully, "I dozed off to sleep while my bedside light was still on. But it was off when he left."

"Are you sure it was a man?" la señora inquired.

"Yes. I could feel the hair on his arms, and the muscles."

"That's not necessarily proof," Miguel volunteered. "Any athletic woman has muscular arms — and hair on her arms."

"Ay, Miguel," la señora chastised. "There is a difference in the size of the arms, and in the amount of hair. Jeannine would have known if it were a woman who held the pillow."

"The lawyer in the family," John said with a sardonic gleam in his eyes. "Okay, it was a man. At least, that's the logical assumption for the moment. But why? Why would some guy climb up to your window and try to suffocate you?"

"I-I don't know. . . ." she replied simply. "Why have any of these things happened around here?"

"Perhaps the assailant thought he was in my room," Doña Josefina offered. "Perhaps you were not the intended victim, Jeannine."

"That's quite likely," Miguel chimed in, his dark face mulling over that possibility.

"But my light was on," Jeannine protested. "He must have seen that I had red hair, that I didn't look anything like Doña Josefina."

"Why do you suppose he turned it off, then?" John asked.

"And why do you suppose that it was turned off at all?" Miguel countered. He walked over to the nightstand and turned the knob at the base of the lamp. Nothing happened. He turned it again, and a third time. Then he looked up and smiled at Jeannine. "The bulb's burned out. It was probably out before your attacker arrived."

"Oh," Jeannine said, feebly.

"You see, then someone could have thought he was in my room, could have been trying to kill me . . . not you."

"I suppose," Jeannine began, then broke into tears again.

La señora waved the men out of the room, and took Jeannine into her thin, frail arms. "It has been a terrible time for you, *niña*. But it will soon be over. Now we must call in the police. . . ."

Chapter 14

The police came and listened attentively while Jeannine told her story. They took notes, and in view of her awful experience and the late hour, asked her to come down to the station as early as she could the next day to sign a complaint.

"A complaint against whom?" Miguel had asked.

"We'll have to have a complaint on file before we can officially begin to question suspects. From what you've all said, having Miss Wellman sign the complaint might keep reporters off the de Lorca back, if you know what I mean."

"Preposterous!" la señora replied. "It's sufficient that Jeannine lives here to get them all interested."

Miguel had shrugged. "Well, it's worth a try."

"Yeah, well once we've got a signed complaint, my men can get to work on finding out who's behind all these accidents. Sure wished you'd called me right after the attempt on John's life, Mrs. de Lorca. That would've made my job a lot easier."

"There's no reason to think it really was an attempt to murder me, officer," John said in his usual offhand way. "It could have been some kid trying to load a rifle and it went off; then he got scared and didn't dare come see if he'd killed me or not."

"Yeah," the policeman said. "Could've been. But it'll be damned — sorry, Mrs. de Lorca — darned hard to find anyone or prove anything now. You gotta get on these things right away before anybody's got a chance to wipe up the evidence."

A few more asides were exchanged, and the policemen left. A heavy silence remained in the living room after their departure, as if none of them wished to say anything lest it create even more tension. But Jeannine was still deeply confused about her assailant, still not quite ready to accept the theory that she had not been the target of the attempted murder. And she was now totally convinced, regardless of what anyone might say, that coincidence was ridiculous. By no stretch of the imagination could these events not have been planned. Much as her gentle nature loathed the idea of violence, she had to face the facts.

"*Bueno,*" la señora said in a tired, labored voice, "we had best get some sleep if we are to face tomorrow with any dignity at all."

"Who can sleep after tonight?" Miguel muttered, yet stood to aid his great-grand-mother out of her favorite high-backed chair.

La señora smiled patiently. "Only the young feel they are missing something while they sleep," she intoned. "It is not how much life one witnesses, but the quality of one's life. Sleep will make us all feel better, and I for one intend to take a sleeping draught."

Jeannine watched Miguel walking beside his grandmother with mixed emotions. How easy it was to pontificate when one became older! She was glad that at least Miguel re-alized sleep would not come easily to some-one who has just had her life threatened. Even as the thought crossed her mind, Miguel turned and paused for a second.

"I'll get one of her pills for you, Jeannine. You'll probably need it."

Chata and Manuel were standing in their nightclothes at the foot of the stairs. As soon as Doña Josefina was abreast of them, Chata took over and helped the woman up-stairs. Manuel stood by almost helplessly, looking almost lost without the faithful Hans at his side. Almost at the same time, both Miguel and Jeannine exclaimed, "The dogs! Where were they tonight!"

By the time Miguel had thrown open the front door, Jeannine was beside him. He whistled into the black night, softly at first, then more shrilly demanding as his whistles met with no response.

Jeannine, chilled to the marrow as she stood in the doorway, called to each of the dogs by name. There was a sense of doom in the cold, damp night air; a feeling of hopelessness as they each tried to summon the German shepherds.

"You stay here," Miguel whispered to her.

"Where are you going?"

"To find the dogs!"

With that, he strode into the darkness, calling out Hans and Bruno softly until he was too far from the house for her to hear him any longer. Jeannine felt useless just standing there, torn between running after Miguel to be with him and yet somehow afraid to go out there, out into the enveloping darkness, the fears of the night still with her. What if her assailant were lurking behind a tree? What if all of this had been prearranged? Timidly, chastising herself as all manner of coward, Jeannine returned to the living room to await Miguel. If only he'd taken a flashlight with him . . . something to light the way so he could see the dogs — or whatever else that might lie in wait in the moonless darkness.

No one remained in the living room, and Jeannine assumed that John had gone up to bed. There was such a deadly stillness in the room that she could hear the whistle of silence within her head. Somewhere in the house there should be a sound; John dropping a slipper, la señora leaning on her cane as she climbed into bed, or Chata and Manuel speaking in lowered tones — a sound of some sort. Yet there was nothing.

Only two lamps had been lighted while the police had been there. The lamps now cast eerie shadows against drapes that seemed to pulsate with a throbbing life of their own; menacing, undulating rhythms inside the heavy folds of the draperies. A window creaked ominously as the branch of a tree brushed against it, and Jeannine found herself curling into an embryonic position, burying herself more deeply into the cushions of the wing-back chair.

She felt eyes upon her; sensed someone watching her . . . watching . . . waiting. . . . As if all her fears were now coming to the surface of her consciousness, she felt a coldness, a clamminess creeping into the room. Her mind strained for the least small sound, as if half expecting to feel strong fingers entwine about her throat. In her head, the name and image of Miguel would not disappear.

Miguel had been the only one in the entire household who had not had any accidents . . . Miguel had not been in the car when it had gone off the road . . . Miguel, or someone who sounded like him, had been in the attic the night she fell down the stairs . . . Miguel had not been present when the sniper had fired . . . and Miguel had not been the intended victim of some murderer.

At any one of the occasions, Miguel could easily have been the cause or source of each of the accidents. He could have hired someone to tinker with the car, or perhaps even have done it himself. Maybe he had played upon Manuel's intense loyalty to Doña Josefina to do something to the car, which Manuel certainly would know how to do. Miguel could have loosened the tile, too. After each occasion, Miguel had made a great display of concern and of looking for the causes for them — perhaps too great a display? Perhaps he was only trying to seem concerned in order to cover his own tracks?

Miguel had supposedly been with la señora when the sniper had fired — but was he? Could he not have slipped out? Would it not be possible for the sniper to be Miguel? And tonight? A man's hands on the pillow . . . with fine hairs on his arms. His arms, she thought, squeezing her eyes shut tightly trying to recapture what she'd felt, his arms had been bare — not even a watch. Miguel never wore a wristwatch; instead he carried his father's pocket watch. Her assailant had not worn a watch . . . she was certain of that!

Anyone attempting to murder Doña Josefina would be sure to know where she slept, wouldn't he? And surely, even in the dark, any murderer trying to kill la señora would have known he had the wrong person simply by the force of Jeannine's struggle — la señora would never have that kind of strength! Even Doña Josefina must have realized that! Why then would she have even suggested that Jeannine was not the intended victim? To calm Jeannine's fears? To protect someone? To protect Miguel?

While these damning thoughts reverberated through Jeannine's mind, a loping wind had risen outside and a damp drizzle had settled upon the foliage surrounding the house. It altered the sounds about her, it altered the stillness. Leaves scraped against windowpanes like sandpaper, and the floorboards of the house constricted, creaking or snapping with the damp that seeped in. Fear spread through her body like seaweed brought in with the tide, floating listlessly on the surface of her consciousness. Was it her unknown fear of Miguel that had stopped her from going with him to find the dogs? Had some inner voice warned her just in time, before she found herself out in the night, alone with Miguel?

"If there is nothing else, señorita . . ."

The sound of a man's voice nearly paralyzed Jeannine with terror. It cracked through her senses like summer lightning when there wasn't a cloud in sight. It was only with the greatest effort that Jeannine was able to pull herself together and recognize Manuel standing in the doorway. Her pulse still pounding in her ears, she managed to acknowledge Manuel's query. "No, thank you, Manuel . . . I won't need anything else."

"Then, *buenas noches,* señorita." He turned in the darkened doorway and disappeared into the foyer.

Still trembling with the shock of Manuel's appearance, she strove to think more calmly about Miguel, about what was happening at "Puerta de Paz."

Why *should* Miguel have any wish to cause any of them harm? There was no apparent reason. He doted upon his great-grandmother: Why? From genuine love, or

191

for his inheritance? Was he telling the truth when he said no one knew the contents of la señora's will? That Miguel had no use for his cousins John and Olga was glaringly obvious — would a man plotting murder be so open about his feelings toward them? Perhaps. Maybe it was the cleverest way of all to throw suspicion off himself when something "accidental" happened to them.

But why should he want to kill her, Jeannine wondered. Why in the world should she become part of the plot? Unless, of course, it was part of Miguel's plan. If he could make people believe that a reign of terror had been instigated by the dam-site backers, that as a member of the household Jeannine had accidently been murdered . . . yes . . . that would be diabolically clever.

The front door was flung open and the wind sliced through the doorway, lifting pages of magazines and flipping through them, fluttering along curtains and lamp-shades, rattling bric-a-brac rudely.

Within seconds Miguel stood inside the foyer, holding the limp form of one of the dogs in his arms. Miguel's dark curly hair lay matted about his forehead, and his face was sleek with the cold drizzle outside. He stood with legs apart, looking very much as if he'd just made a sacrifice of the dog to the gods — and Jeannine sat immobilized with fear as she beheld this man she now doubted so strongly.

"Help me, Jeannine," Miguel said in a low, tired voice. "They're not dead, but I think they've been drugged. We've got to get something warm into them. . . . Who knows how long the brutes have been lying out in this cold night air."

Jeannine hesitated. She was both afraid of Miguel, yet touched by his unexpected concern for the dogs. Could a killer love animals? Yes, she answered herself, which is why he might just drug them and not slit their throats.

"Jeannine, please hurry," he said as he brought the dog into the room and placed him before the hearth. "I'll get Bruno now. Get plenty of blankets from upstairs, Jeannine, and see if there's any broth in the kitchen we can warm up. Quickly."

She rose, almost automatically obeying Miguel's command. Killer or not, Jeannine suddenly knew that she would always obey Miguel's commands. Not because she had to, not even because he expected it; but because she wanted to. *Oh, my God!* Jeannine thought, *you're in love with him, you fool! You're in love with a man who could be a murderer!*

Chapter 15

By the time Jeannine returned to the living room carrying several heavy wool blankets, Miguel had brought in the other dog and stretched him alongside Hans. He had thrown new logs on the fire and had stoked the embers until tongues of flame curled around the dry bark. She stood only a few steps away from Miguel's kneeling form, just looking at him, trying to see some telltale sign that would confirm her worst suspicions about him.

"Don't just stand there," Miguel barked. "Hand me the blankets and then go see about some warm soup."

She responded instantly, turning the heavy blankets over to him and watched momentarily as he spread them across the two prostrate beasts. Jeannine was fascinated by the way Miguel was rubbing their legs and shoulders, forcing circulation into their limbs with his strong masculine hands. He couldn't be a killer! she told herself. He just can't be!

At that moment, Miguel glanced up at

her impatiently while the crackling fire high-lighted his features. His face was perhaps a little too broad, but his brow was straight and firm, his nose chiseled, and his lips were full without being feminine or decadent. There was the look of the devil in Miguel de Lorca, an expression of someone pos-sessed or burdened; but not the look of a killer.

"Jeannine," he said after a moment, his voice calm but firm, "I know you've had an exhausting night . . . but the dogs will die if you don't help me now. We can't just let them die without trying to save them."

Her response was a shy, slightly embar-rassed smile, and without another thought she ran to the kitchen. Jeannine found the light switch without difficulty, and as quietly as she could she lifted the lid from an earth-enware bowl on the stove. Good old Chata, she thought as she gazed into the pot and saw a chicken carcass resting in the broth, no one can accuse Chata of wasting la señora's household monies!

Jeannine searched in a few cupboards un-til she found the pots and pans, then ladled out several cups of the broth and put a low flame beneath the pan. She knew from her orphanage days that a slow flame brought out the most flavor and aroma, and since

Jeannine had never heard of German shepherds eating chicken soup, she deduced she'd need all the advantages she could muster. As soon as it was warmed, she brought the pan and two teaspoons back to the living room where Miguel was still rubbing the animals' limbs.

Silently, they each spoon-fed the supine dogs. Neither of them really knew how, but they managed by trial and error to get the broth down. Bruno roused first, a small whimper low in his throat.

Pleased with their success, Miguel smiled into Jeannine's eyes. Then he looked down at Bruno and said, "He doesn't look much like a trained killer now, does he?"

Her immediate reaction was to think that neither did Miguel, but she hated herself for even letting the idea enter her head. Miguel was not the guilty one; he couldn't be.

The sky had turned gray, heralding the dawn, before Hans, too, was revived. Now Miguel slumped, visibly tired, on the floor with his back resting against the settee. One hand rested on Bruno while he laid his head back against the cushion.

Jeannine was so tired by then that she was almost beyond realizing it. Stretched out with her body curled around Hans to keep him warm, her head propped up by her hand, she let herself be mesmerized by the waning fire. She looked over at Miguel and wondered if he'd fallen asleep. Jeannine noted the growth of beard on his face and couldn't resist smiling to herself; she had never seen him when he wasn't clean-shaven, and she fleetingly wondered if she would ever see him this way again.

"Are you cold, Jeannine?" Miguel asked softly, not moving his head from its resting place.

"No," she replied lazily. "I think Hans is keeping me warmer than I'm keeping him. They're really beautiful dogs, aren't they?" she added.

Miguel brought his gaze to rest upon her and she met it. His eyes were tired, but none of the fire had gone out of them.

"You've really been wonderful, Jeannine. I'm sorry I was barking orders at you earlier, but . . ."

"Don't be silly, Miguel. I was absolutely in a stupor when you showed up holding Hans in your arms."

Miguel's hand moved away from the dog's sleeping form to take Jeannine's and hold it firmly. His large hand was warm and his grip was strong yet gentle. "You're a very remarkable young lady. Not many women would have hung around this house with all that's been going on."

"Stubborn, that's what I am," she said, trying to make light of his remark.

"No," he contradicted. "You're loyal, and brave, and very, very lovely."

She didn't know what to say, but it didn't seem to matter while he held her hand so tightly.

"John's in love with you, you know that, don't you?" Miguel made the announcement so softly she could barely hear him. "I suppose he's proposed to you. . . ."

"No," Jeannine answered, almost as softly as he. "I don't think John's really in love with me at all."

"Why do you say that? I know John quite well; I know the signs when he's smitten."

"Smitten?" Jeannine had to laugh at the archaic term, and how typical it was of Miguel to use it. "Well, perhaps that, but not in love. He's really looking for a playmate, that's all."

It was Miguel's turn to laugh. "How did you figure that out, Jeannine Wellman?"

She shrugged; she wasn't going to tell Miguel about the scene with John.

Miguel, still smiling, leaned forward toward Jeannine and gently pulled her reclining body up to where he sat. "And my

198

grandmother thinks you're the most wonderful thing since Cortez conquered Mexico."

"Has she said so?" Jeannine asked, pleased to her toes.

"Well, words to that effect," Miguel amended.

Her face was resting on his chest, rising and falling with every breath he took. She could even hear his heartbeat through his clothes and was surprised at how strong and steady it was. There was something so right about the moment and their closeness that it didn't occur to her to be elated or excited about their proximity. She had not really thought about such a moment with Miguel, but then, here they were, their arms about each other. The hours they had just spent together, this moment of tenderness between them, seemed idyllic to her — perhaps heightened by her earlier speculations about Miguel, but she thought not. It was an emotion born of acceptance of another human being, with faults and frailties, but also with strengths and manliness. And Jeannine wholly accepted that she loved Miguel as a complete human being. He was real, she loved him, and she accepted him.

Even as these realizations raced through her mind, he bent his head and placed his lips on hers. She gave herself up to his kiss. The outline of his lips pressed softly against her, his free hand touching her face in light caresses. Jeannine had never been kissed so tenderly, so lovingly.

When he broke their embrace, she was startled to see the expression in his eyes; he looked as if he were in great pain. "I'm sorry, Jeannine. I shouldn't have done that."

"But . . ." she began to protest.

"No! I'm sorry. It won't happen again. You'd better go up to your room now and get some rest. I'll stay with the dogs."

Jeannine wanted to cry out, to scream at this man that she loved him — but her pride wouldn't let her. Enraged, feeling brutally rejected, she stormed from the room and went upstairs. As she crawled beneath the warm covers of her own bed, tears of hurt frustration welled up in her eyes and tumbled down her cheek to the pillow. "Oh, *damn* him!" she cursed softly. "What an impossible, rigid, domineering, selfish . . . *oh!*"

Chapter 16

It was late morning before Jeannine, escorted by Doña Josefina and a very silent Miguel, arrived at the police station to file her complaint with Officer Shroyer. Miguel told the policeman about the dogs, and a vet was dispatched to take blood samples.

"It's too soon for us to have much information for you, Miss Wellman, but one nice thing about small town life is a small population. It's pretty hard to keep anything a secret around here. We'll get him, don't you worry."

Doña Josefina glowered at Officer Shroyer as if he were some cardboard hero out of a TV series, but for once, said nothing. They returned to the house completely immersed in their own individual thoughts, a barrier of introspection laying heavily between them.

Jeannine was too emotionally and physically exhausted to even try to sort out her thoughts. All she could really do was hope to keep her eyes open until they returned to the house, where she could excuse herself to go to bed for a nap. If anyone had told her a year before that staying up all night would have such a devastating effect upon her, she'd have denied it vehemently. But then, she conceded, it wasn't the staying up; it was the horrible experience, and the emotional strain of what had happened later after Miguel had kissed her. Why, oh, why had he kissed her and then retreated so abruptly! Did he think that she returned John's affections and that he was trespassing? Miguel had some rather old-fashioned notions, but surely he didn't think that! But Jeannine was too weary for logic. She was merely reacting, not reasoning. She hoped some rest would clear her mind.

When Manuel pulled the vintage Cadillac before the front door, the three alighted with leaden movements. Miguel opened the door for the two women and then hovered briefly over la señora. "I'll phone you several times every day to be sure you're all right," he said, then placed a light kiss on her forehead.

"We'll be all right, Miguel, *no te preocupes.*"

Jeannine suddenly realized that Miguel's suitcase was standing near the front door, and that this was his farewell. She was too disoriented to know quite what to do or say. Jeannine glanced from Miguel to la señora to the suitcase and back again, wondering what it was all about. Before she could get her wits about her, Miguel had picked up his valise and was climbing back into the Cadillac. She felt herself rising up on her toes, as if to call after him, and instead silently watched the car pull away on the gravel, heading back down the mountain.

La señora placed a cool, parchment-dry hand on her forearm. "He has gone to Monterey, even as we discussed it. I'm sure you will miss him, *niña,* but it has to be done this way."

"But so soon?" Her voice sounded distant and alien to her.

"Yes. The sooner the better. It must be thus if we are to smoke out who is behind all of this. John, of course, will leave this afternoon." Jeannine was not in the least interested in John's comings and goings, but it was incredible to her that Miguel could leave like that without even a word to her, without their having even five minutes to discuss what had happened between them. It was too cruel this way, too hard to know what to think or do.

"But . . ."

"You are tired, my dear. Please go to your room and get some rest before lunch is served. We'll talk about it then."

Numbly, Jeannine complied. She felt as if her whole world had collapsed, as if nothing made sense any longer, as if the fates had turned against her. Her body was drained of energy as she lumbered up the stairs; her mind felt like a thick, dull slab of granite. She had to admit, if only to herself, that much of her extreme fatigue was due to her rheumatic condition. She had not been getting enough rest, and the strain of the past few weeks was beginning to tell on her. The tightness in her chest, the shortness of breath, the feeling that any exertion at all was more than she could bear; all of these were but hints and warnings from her body to slow up, to take better care of herself. It was bad enough to be under such tension, but not to have enough sleep in addition was inviting another attack.

Well, now that Miguel and John would be away, perhaps the entire matter would be resolved. Now that the police had been formally brought into the case, surely the nightmare would come to an end.

As she reached the upstairs hallway, she heard the door to John's bedroom open. He opened the door wide and stood watching her weary progress. "I guess you already know that the old lady is throwing me out today," he said.

Jeannine struggled to draw a deep breath, to get some strong, clean air into her lungs. "I strongly doubt that you can call it being thrown out," she said after a moment, pausing at the top of the stairs with her small hand gripping the railing. "Miguel's already left," she added. "And you did agree to this plan, John. You know you did." She was really too tired to get into a discussion with John, to be patient and understanding; but she didn't know how to cut off the conversation. It would have been unforgivably rude.

"Well, I don't mind especially. I've already stayed a lot longer than I usually would." He grinned at her impishly. "And, too, I'm getting just a little bored with all these damned melodramatic accidents. Especially since I seem to always be right in the middle of them."

Exhaustion brought a sudden flush to Jeannine's cheeks, and she momentarily felt faint, teetering slightly on her feet. Instantly John rushed to her side and placed his arms around her for support. "Oh, darling! I'm sorry, so very sorry," he whispered in her ear. "Here I am, rattling on about myself, when you're the one who's had the worst of it all!"

While Jeannine was glad she'd not said

anything harsh to him, she still had a very good idea of just how deeply John's contrition went. With what little strength she still possessed, she managed to extricate herself from his embrace. "Your grandmother's right, John. With you and Miguel out of the house, perhaps we'll be able to narrow down the source of these events. I'm sure you'll not be the victim once you're back in San Francisco, surrounded by your beautiful friends and going to all your beautiful places."

John's expression clouded instantly. "Well surely you don't think that anyone else is the victim! I mean, yes, you've been inconvenienced — to say the least — by what someone's trying to do to *me*, but let's not forget who they really want to get rid of!"

"Oh, John. Just a few days ago you were emphatically denying that you had any enemies who'd want to cause you harm. Now you're convinced that someone's out to get you?"

John straightened up haughtily. "I suppose you think you are?"

"I am what?" Jeannine asked wearily.

"The victim."

"John, if it makes you feel better to think that there's a conspiracy against you, believe me . . . it's all yours. I don't want it. All I want to do is go to my room and get some rest."

"Well, of all the selfish . . . Listen, Jeannie, I was going to ask you to come with me to San Francisco. To get out of this mausoleum and be with people your own age. I'd hoped that once I got you away from here, I could convince you that I loved you, and that we could . . ."

"Could what? Could get married?" She couldn't resist the opportunity to remind him that she was not like his other women friends, that she didn't go to bed with just any man because she'd taken a fancy to him.

"Or just live together," he said with a grin. "Maybe you'd buy a dress before you had tried it on, but I like to know what I'm getting into."

She ignored his teasing. "John, please don't talk about any of that now. You go on back to your friends. I have a job here. I have become extremely fond of your great-grandmother, and I think that I could live here in Carmel for the rest of my life. People my own age do not necessarily make the best friends. If you're sincere in your feelings about me, you'd also know that you and I could never be happy together. We just don't see things the same way. I hate parties, I hate crowds, I hate big cities. . . ."

"But you don't hate me, do you?" he interrupted, almost sheepishly.

Jeannine smiled and touched his face with her palm. "No, John. I don't. But I could never be your wife, and I've no desire to be your mistress."

"Is it Miguel? Is he why you're not interested in me?"

Jeannine looked at John; looked directly into his boyish, inquiring eyes. "At this moment, I'm not interested in anyone. And if I were, I wouldn't tell you. Now may I go to my room?"

He stared at her as if trying to read her mind, trying to see into her soul, but apparently gave it up. "Promise me you'll take care of yourself?" he asked quietly.

Jeannine nodded, a forgiving smile on her lips. "I promise."

John bent forward and kissed her on the cheek. "I'll miss you," he said.

"And you'll get over it," she answered with a light laugh.

"Probably," he agreed. "Phone me if you need me for anything."

"Have a good trip, John. And try not to borrow any more money from anyone," she said with an amused tone in her voice.

He grinned. "You're right, we'd never make it together."

She watched him as he went back to his room. Even from where she stood, Jeannine could see his suitcase on the bed, his clothes balled up and jammed inside with about as much premeditated organization as a hurricane. She shook her head and walked down the hall to her own room. Once inside, she locked the window that her attacker had used, then crossed over to the other wall and opened the windows that faced out to sea. Whoever it was, she thought, he'd better have wings if he wants to get through this window!

Jeannine slept all afternoon, right through the lunch hour. When she awoke, it was dusk. Guiltily, she bathed and dressed for dinner, then rushed downstairs hoping against hope that Doña Josefina was not angry with her. The doors to the living room were closed, and she could dimly make out voices. She rapped lightly, then went in. "Dr. Sternig!" she exclaimed the moment she saw him.

He came forward with long strides. "Hello, my dear."

"But you weren't expected until Monday," she said, pleasure etched across her otherwise drawn face.

"Well, as it turns out, I'll have to be testifying in an accident case on Monday. I had a chance to get up here today, so I called Mrs. de Lorca —"

"And I asked him to rush right up," la señora finished for him. "How are you, *niña?* Feeling a little better now that you've had some rest?"

Jeannine smiled her assurance that she was feeling much better, but she was not unaware of the professional way in which Dr. Sternig was looking at her. "How long can you stay?" she asked.

They returned to the center of the room and sat down together on the sofa facing la señora. "I've booked a room at the hotel," he said.

"Nonsense!" Mrs. de Lorca exclaimed. "You shall stay here tonight." She banged her cane against the floor, and as soon as Manuel appeared, she ordered him to phone the hotel and cancel the doctor's reservation, and dispatched Manuel to fetch his luggage. "We've had two men in this house for several weeks now, and they both just left today. It will be nice to have a gentleman in the house to help us make an adjustment," she said.

Jeannine found it difficult to keep from

showing her surprise at how gracious la señora was being. Either Doña Josefina had taken quite a liking to Dr. Vincent Sternig, or she was bending over backwards to show Jeannine that "Puerta de Paz" was truly her home, that any friend of Jeannine's was more than merely welcome. Either way, Jeannine was delighted.

They dined that evening speaking of just about everything except the events that had transpired recently. Jeannine had to assume that la señora had apprised the doctor of the happenings before Jeannine joined them. It was, to her relief, a pleasure to see the doctor, and to talk of things in Los Angeles. She was smugly pleased to hear that they'd been having some bad days of smog, that traffic only got worse, and that there was a gasoline shortage.

La señora, on the other hand, listened to the news of Los Angeles as if listening to a Martian news broadcast. It was appalling to her that any intelligent human being would endure such living conditions.

Jeannine was not unaware of how Doña Josefina was taking it all in; her eyes would spark with outrage, or squint with incredulity. Several times, the woman seemed about to make one of her devastating, leveling remarks, but then thought better of it and said nothing — an expression of prudence veiling her face. Jeannine would have smiled on these occasions, but she didn't dare let la señora know that she was aware of the woman's tact for her benefit. It was enough that Doña Josefina was making such a monumental effort to not reveal her outrageous domineering side. Jeannine was terribly touched, and very pleased with the way la señora was restraining herself on Jeannine's behalf.

Ultimately, over coffee, the subject of Jeannine's health came up, and it was decided that the doctor would give her an examination first thing in the morning. He had to be back in Los Angeles by two in the afternoon, and he planned to drive his rented car back to San Francisco and fly down from there.

When la señora excused herself to retire, Dr. Sternig lit up a cigar and leaned back, toying with the coffee spoon before him. "She's quite a woman, your Doña Josefina," he said casually.

"You don't even know the half of it," Jeannine said. "She was on good behavior tonight — for your sake, I think, as much as mine."

He laughed. "Yes, I can see that it would be unwise to cross her path."

There was only a moment's pause when Jeannine blurted out, "How old would you say she was?"

"Hmm, I don't know. It's hard to tell, really. She could be eighty-five or ninety. Hasn't she told you?"

"No. Not a word."

"That's rather unusual. The older people get, once they're past seventy, anyway, the more they like to talk about their ages. I suppose it's some sort of pride in their endurance, their longevity. But usually you can't get them off the subject."

"Did you notice her eyes?"

"Yes, of course. How could anyone not notice them! There's certainly no senility involved; she's as sharp as a scalpel!"

Manuel entered the dining room silently, bowing to the doctor as he approached, but looking at Jeannine. "Would *el doctor* enjoy more wine? Perhaps some brandy?"

Jeannine glanced at him, received his affirmation, and relayed it to Manuel. When Manuel left the room and they were alone again, she raised the glass in toast. "To 'Puerta de Paz,' " she said.

"And may peace and harmony be restored," he added.

Jeannine gazed at Dr. Sternig for a few seconds. "She told you, then?"

"Yes. Now *you* tell me. It doesn't sound very good."

She leaned back heavily against the ornately scrolled dining chair. "I don't think there's much else to tell you," she said softly. "And I'm certainly not the one to fill you in, Dr. Sternig. I don't know anything more than you do, or the man in the moon for that matter."

Dr. Sternig blew out a blue ring of smoke, stared at its disintegration, then looked directly into Jeannine's eyes. "You sound rather bitter — no, that's too strong. Frustrated; yes, frustrated."

Jeannine had to smile at herself. "Well, I *am*." She then proceeded to tell the doctor about the events that had occurred, about Dr. Franklin and "the feud" no one would discuss, and even about the dogs. She hesitated, however, whenever any of the information might seem to implicate Miguel as the possible culprit. Even though she herself couldn't, wouldn't, believe Miguel capable of such deeds, Jeannine was not a fool; others, not influenced by love, might well think otherwise. When she'd finished giving her account, she glanced down at her hands and was shocked to see that they were trembling.

"Is that just tension," Dr. Sternig asked,

nodding toward her hands, "or are you genuinely afraid?"

"Both, I suppose," she replied. "Having someone trying to kill one of us is not my idea of a serene life."

"And I'm sure that having someone trying to smother you in your sleep didn't do much to improve your nerves."

"No. Of course not. And I just don't buy la señora's theory that it was really she he was after!"

"Tell me," he began slowly, calmly. "What about these two great-grandchildren, John and Miguel? What are they like?"

Jeannine thought about his question for a moment, then laughed. "They're about as alike as chili peppers and watermelon!" she said. "John's in his early thirties. He's handsome and dashing, a jetset playboy when he can afford it — and even when he can't — and he's about as responsible as a kleptomaniac locked in a department store overnight."

"Well, now," the doctor grinned, "that's a rather vivid picture of the fellow. But he doesn't sound like someone to be considered dangerous."

"I don't think John could harm a fly."

"And Miguel?"

Jeannine's eyes veiled subconsciously; she

found herself unable to really discuss him. "The opposite. He's a year or two older, very dark, very serious."

"And dangerous?" Dr. Sternig prompted softly.

"No! Of course not!" Jeannine protested immediately. "He's just, well, Miguel's just not like John at all. Is that so terrible? Does being serious make one dangerous?"

"All right," Dr. Sternig said, throwing his hands up in the air in surrender. He leaned forward, stamped out his cigar, then instantly lighted a fresh one. "I smoke too much," he muttered to himself, then lapsed into awkward silence.

Neither of them seemed quite sure of what to do or say for a few moments. Jeannine's mind was in a turmoil and for the first time since early that afternoon, she realized how very empty the house seemed without Miguel's presence, and a sense of loneliness crept into her heart as she wondered how long it would be before she would see him again . . . if she would ever see him again.

"I see," Dr. Sternig said, apparently apropos of nothing in particular.

"What?" Jeannine asked, forcing her thoughts back to the present.

"You're in love with Miguel."

Her eyes glistened with tears she would not permit herself. "Yes."

"Does he know?"

"I'm not sure."

Dr. Sternig placed one large warm hand over hers. "Is he in love with you?"

"I-I'm not sure."

"Well, young lady, it would seem as if the only thing you can be sure about around here is that there's an unknown evil around 'Puerta de Paz' and an inordinate amount of mystery."

"And that I'm deeply in love with a man I hardly know."

Dr. Sternig smiled reassuringly, affectionately. "That's no mystery, Jeannine, that's chemistry."

Chapter 17

The physical examination that Dr. Sternig gave Jeannine the next day was quick and relatively simple. Again he admonished her that her health was in serious jeopardy if she didn't take better care of herself. Her pulse was entirely too fast, her nerves were jangled, and the pressures around her were only making matters worse. Naturally, as she'd expected, Dr. Sternig had advised her to pack up and leave Carmel. What she had not expected was his understanding of her love for Miguel. "Of course you won't follow my advice while there's a chance you'll be seeing Miguel," he had said. "But do try to calm down. If there are any more of these attempts at murder — anyone's murder — I won't vouch for how well you'll survive the attack it would be bound to induce."

She had tried to assure the doctor that now that the two men were out of the house, she was rather confident that the tensions would disappear. But she didn't really believe herself, and neither did Dr. Sternig. Once the examination was over, they both met with Dr. Ortíz and thanked him for the use of his offices. Dr. Sternig gave Dr. Ortíz a run-down on Jeannine's medical history, bringing him up to date on what medications he had prescribed in the past, her allergies, and informed Dr. Ortíz of his opinion about her heart condition in view of the terrible strain she had endured while at the hacienda. Dr. Ortíz nodded, made a few notes for his files, and promised to take very good care of Jeannine.

All three of them walked out into the bright sunlight on Guadalupe Street, saying their good-byes affably and oblivious of the pedestrians en route to collect their mail at the post office on Delores Street, where the local residents gathered every day to exchange gossip or news. The smell of pine hung heavily in the air except when the occasional breeze came in from the ocean and filled their nostrils with refreshing salt air.

Dr. Ortíz was formal, but more cordial than Jeannine had ever seen him before. He even smiled twice, which surprised Jeannine as much as if she'd witnessed Doña Josefina leap up to do a flamenco dance. Finally, with Manuel holding the Cadillac door open for them, Jeannine and Dr. Sternig departed for the hacienda. There la señora had an early lunch awaiting them prior to the doctor's return to San Francisco.

By the time Vincent Sternig drove off, la señora had also been given a complete rundown on Jeannine's health. Jeannine began to feel as if she were on public display, but she also knew that Dr. Sternig was only acting out of great affection and concern for her. He gave her a fatherly kiss before he left, and extracted a promise from her to write to him and keep him informed of what was finally learned about the events that had occurred at "Puerta de Paz."

Fortunately, la señora had a good deal of dictation on that day and Jeannine was kept busy for the balance of the afternoon. She barely had a moment to think about herself . . . or Miguel. Of the several phone calls that came through that afternoon, she knew that one of them was from Miguel simply by the way Doña Josefina spoke. Jeannine waited to hear if Miguel would pass along any word for her, any slight phrase that would indicate he was thinking of her. Even something as uninspired as "Say hello to Jeannine for me" would have sufficed; but when la señora returned the receiver to its cradle, she merely put her glasses back on and returned to reading a report on plankton. Jeannine was terribly disappointed, but there was little she could do about it.

Later that evening, after dinner, Jeannine and la señora went to the living room to read for a few hours before bedtime. It seemed so strange to be in that large room, just the two of them. Jeannine rather imagined that parents might feel the same way the first few days after the children have been sent off to camp. She half expected to hear John's bouncing step, or Miguel's rumbling voice talking about some client. Instead, there was only quiet.

As if echoing her thoughts, la señora looked up from her book and gazed out the French windows momentarily. "It is too quiet in here, don't you think?"

"We're used to having company," Jeannine said.

Doña Josefina harrumphed with amusement. "Miguel is company . . . Juanillo is a distraction. Never mind. Why don't you put on the radio, *niña?* Perhaps some soothing music would help us accustom ourselves to their absence."

Jeannine did as she requested, finding a station that was playing Vivaldi's *Four Seasons,* then returned to her chair. She gave up trying to read, accepting that her mind simply wasn't concentrating on the words but kept conjuring up images of Miguel. Instead, she took out her beginner's needlepoint kit and tried to concentrate on the problems of mastering manual dexterity.

When the music ended, the announcer came on with a brief commercial, and then it was time for the nine o'clock news. The farm workers' strike was becoming more hostile, Cambodia was still a hotbed of violence, the problem with the Arab world over oil continued, and sundry other urgent matters of world importance were pronounced, followed by yet another commercial. "On the local scene," the newscaster resumed, "the body of a Los Angeles physician was discovered between Monterey and Carmel today. . . ."

Both Jeannine and la señora sat bolt upright at those words, their eyes locking in fearful disbelief.

"Turn it up, turn it up!" la señora commanded.

". . . There was no apparent motive behind the murder. . . ."

"Murder!" Doña Josefina exclaimed.

". . . a side road not far from the Del Monte turnoff. The car had been set afire, but an autopsy has revealed that the physician had been fatally shot prior to the fire. . . ."

"Oh, my God!" Jeannine whispered. "It can't be!"

"Carajo! Porqué no dicen su nombre?"

At that moment, Manuel came bursting into the room, so obviously upset that the two women felt obligated to calm him rather than listen to the radio. *"El doctor!"* Manuel gushed. "Your Dr. Sternig, he has been killed," he blurted. "It is even just now on the television. . . ."

"Are you sure it was Dr. Sternig?" la señora asked, a deadly calm in her voice.

"Sí, sí! They gave his name!"

Jeannine sank into the nearest chair, her knees buckling under her. "My fault," she muttered inanely to herself. "It's all my fault!" She looked to la señora hopefully.

La señora turned and stared at Jeannine, an expression of sympathy on her face, but for once she had no words of solace. Instead, staring right through Jeannine as if she weren't there, she clutched her cane till her aged, gnarled knuckles were whitely taut and brought it down on the floor with surprising strength. "Now he has gone too far! He has brought his own hell upon himself!" she said tightly, in a barely audible voice.

Jeannine tossed fitfully in her sleep, rousing from time to time as if sensing some terrible danger near at hand. The horror of Dr. Sternig's murder still plagued her. And la señora's words upon the news of his death reverberated throughout Jeannine's consciousness. Who had "gone too far" and who had brought hell upon himself? She had wanted to ask even at the time, but hadn't dared; and too, she rationalized, she'd been too shocked at the news, too filled with an overwhelming sense of guilt, to question Doña Josefina further. She still couldn't quite believe it — why? Why would anyone want to murder him? It was bizarre! Too much was happening; too much violence, too much hatred. Jeannine felt surrounded by hostility, by some ubiquitous enemy determined to destroy not only her, but everything around her. And now, in the deadly hostile atmosphere of her darkened bedroom, she knew without any doubt that it was she who was the victim.

She didn't know why; she almost didn't care. But obviously la señora knew a good deal more than she had revealed previously. She knew *who* . . . and that was probably more important than the why. Despite the sleeping pill la señora had given her, Jeannine was too horrified, too upset to sleep. She sat up and turned on her bedside lamp, hoping that the light would help dispel her fears. For once in her life she wished she smoked; perhaps it would help calm her.

Yet even as that thought crossed her mind, questions she wanted to put to Doña Josefina de Lorca gnawed at her; and no sooner would these questions take form in her mind, than her thoughts would return to Miguel. Miguel! Again, he had had the opportunity . . . and Miguel lived in Monterey; knew that Dr. Sternig had been there, because Jeannine had overheard la señora tell him just before dinner on the day that the doctor had first arrived.

Jeannine sat in bed trembling with the fear of the unknown, with the dreaded cognizance of Miguel's guilt. It was more than she could endure. Murder attempts that were possibly nothing more than scare tactics . . . this she might be able to accept, to forgive — but cold-blooded murder of a man who had nothing to do with anything that was happening in Carmel or the Carmel Valley? It was psychotic . . . and it was breaking her spirit. She loved Miguel desperately — could she love such a man? Would there not be other signs of cruelty and selfishness? Would there not be some frenzied gleam in his eyes? Something? *Anything* that would indicate Miguel was capable of such behavior?

Glancing at the small clock beside the lamp, she dimly realized that it was two in

225

the morning. The information passed into and out of her mind the way one might note a speck of lint and swiftly forget it. She had to talk to la señora . . . and at once. Jeannine could not stand even one more second of this torment! If Doña Josefina had the answer, then Jeannine would extract it from her before the night was out, even if she had to shake it out of her!

Jeannine slipped on her robe and slippers and padded into the hallway toward la señora's room with a purposefulness that was forbidding. As she passed the stairs to the attic, crossing to the opposite end of the hallway, she once again noted the light beneath the door — and heard deep voices. Was Miguel back? she wondered.

The mere thought of his return hastened Jeannine's step. When she reached la señora's door, she rapped but there was no response. She tapped a little harder, but still there was no answer. From many conversations, Jeannine knew perfectly well that la señora was a very light sleeper; surely she had heard! Frantic with worry, she opened the door and stepped into the bedroom.

The bed was turned down, and an indentation showed that the woman had been in it . . . but she was nowhere to be seen now. A single light burned on a bureau in front of a window; the rest of the room was in shadowy darkness. "Mrs. de Lorca?" she called hesitantly.

Like some apparition, la señora stumbled through the open doorway. Robed from throat to floor in a white velvet dressing gown, her white hair untied and hanging to her waist, la señora approached, a knife handle protruding from her abdomen. A dark spreading stain seeped through the material like some growing organism. "Go, *niña!* Go swiftly! He . . . he's here! He wants . . . to . . . kill. . . ."

Even as the words choked in the woman's throat, Jeannine saw the looming bulk of a man approaching them, but it was too dark to make out who it was. The light from the attic stairs was behind him, and all she knew was that it was the killer. They stood across from each other for what seemed like hours, and Jeannine's mind raced with her desperate indecision. La señora was wounded, perhaps mortally — how could she just run away and leave the old woman? She stood frozen, immobilized, not knowing what to do or how to go about it. Even if she wanted to run, how would she get past him?

La señora took the decision out of Jeannine's hands. With some superhuman effort, she threw her frail weight against the man and clung to him as if he were a log in rapids. *"Váyate, niña, antes de que te mate!"*

As if a switch had been thrown, Jeannine responded instantly. Grasping the moment's uncertainty, the bewilderment of their attacker, she rushed past him toward the escape of the stairs. She didn't know what made her move, or how she was managing to run so swiftly down the the stairs and into the foyer; she was like an automaton with a survival instinct.

It seemed only moments before she heard the heavy running steps behind her, coming after her, gaining upon her.

Her heart pounding in her throat, Jeannine unbolted the front door and raced out into the night running wildly, without any true sense of direction. Her every breath felt like a stiletto in her chest as she ran toward the end of the landscaped lawns and toward the edge of the precipice before the sharp descent of the mountainside began. There, she flung herself upon the dew-covered lawn and, tears of terror streaming down her cheeks, she dragged herself beneath a huge bush, hanging onto its thick roots as if she feared she might lose her footing and go over the edge.

Chapter 18

The sliver of a moon shed little light, indicating that the dawn was not too far away. Panting, gasping for air, her head a foundry of angry hammers, Jeannine lay and waited. Every rasping breath she took tore at her aching lungs, and her heart cramped convulsively against her ribs, beating violently. She squinted into the night, trying to see if he had been able to follow her. She peered into the protective darkness, which was equally protective for her pursuer. She waited. Her legs felt wooden, dead, heavy as cast iron. She watched. Nothing.

As she regained her breath, she began to be aware of the sounds of the night. Of the occasional cricket, the fanciful wind through the treetops . . . and she waited.

Jeannine strained to hear something alien to nature, something more than her own heartbeat pulsing in her ears. She realized it was probably silly; who could possibly hear a footfall upon wet grass? Yet, perhaps he would stumble, or snap a fallen twig. She listened, and she waited.

With the cunning born of fear, she knew she could not return to the house, that there was nothing she could do for la señora at that point. She could only hope that Manuel or Chata had heard the commotion and had gone to investigate. But the man who was following her, the man who wanted her dead — he too knew she could not return to the house. He was out there in the night, and he too was waiting, waiting. She didn't dare try to cross the lawn to get away; he could be behind any bush or tree, ready to ambush her the moment she made her whereabouts known. Jeannine reasoned that her only chance for escape was to get to the garage, to the small VW, which always had the keys in the ignition — but how? The garage was at least twenty-five yards from where she crouched beneath the bush, and even so, she'd have to get across the gravel driveway to reach it — would she then be far enough away to have time to open the garage door and drive the car out? What if he were lurking near there? What if he had anticipated her only possible avenue of escape?

Suddenly, she heard a sharp snap followed by a dull thud. Her head whipped toward the sounds, her panic mounting. She wanted desperately to scream, but controlled herself with nerves as fragile as a spider's web. No matter how much she strained to see what had caused the noise, nothing seemed to be other than it should. The wind rose again, and as she looked upward through the trees, she heard the snapping sound again — but this time she saw a pine cone fall to the soft ground. The wind was her enemy on this night. Though perhaps not. Perhaps her murderer would hear the wind sounds, would assume they were her footsteps, and would have gone in another direction from where she lay.

Some inner sense advised her that she had to leave that spot; had to reach the car. She couldn't lie in that same place all night; her pursuer would find her ultimately . . . would find her, and kill her. Even as he had attacked la señora, a helpless old woman. Jeannine's soul cried out in silent prayer that Doña Josefina was all right, that the wound was not mortal; if only she could be *sure* that Manuel had heard the noise, that he'd gone upstairs to see what was happening! The thought of la señora lying on the cold floor, slowly bleeding to death, filled Jeannine with such sadness that she nearly forgot her own peril.

No matter how she looked at it, she had to get to that car — for her own life, and possibly for the life of la señora. She would get to the VW and drive directly to Dr. Franklin's house! He would help her; he would come back with her and save Doña Josefina. He had already proven that he was a doctor first, and an adversary of la señora second; hadn't he come out in the middle of the night to attend to both John and Jeannine after the automobile accident? He'd not permitted their feud to stand in the way of giving medical attention when it was required. Yes, yes, she thought, I've got to get to Dr. Franklin's house!

Without conscious thought, Jeannine slowly began edging her way through the bushes and toward the driveway. She knew that her best route for survival was to remain with the protective bushes. If the wind held, it would be almost impossible for the murderer to hear her movements.

Laboriously, she dragged herself through the dirt and rocky edge of the mountainside, the twigs and thistles of the shrubbery slicing at her tender flesh. She wanted to stand up and run, but knew that would be suicide. Her only chance was to pull herself along through the underbrush. Occasionally, a thorn or twig would dig deeply into her leg, or her arm, and she winced with the pain, knowing she must be bleeding but not daring to stop, not daring to even cry or whimper. Every ten feet or so, she would pause and listen again for a man's footfall, for the sounds of her stalker. Nothing.

As she progressed farther and farther, hearing nothing and seeing nothing, Jeannine began to take courage that she was going to succeed in reaching the car. Heartened, she doubled her efforts, heedless of the way her clothing was being torn and muddied, lightheaded with the promise of escape. Soon she was near enough to the garage to make out its outline in the fading moonlight. With a stifled gasp of relieved joy, she noticed that the doors were already open; she wouldn't have to go through the ordeal of racing against time, in plain view. Thank God! she thought. She had no idea of how careful Manuel usually was about such things, but at the moment she could have hugged him for forgetting to lock up this once!

When Jeannine reached the last shrub before the driveway — what now seemed an awesome expanse — she rested and listened and watched. Her body throbbed with the exertion of dragging her own weight so far and from the multiple bruises and lacerations she had suffered, but now she had hope of success. She'd come all that way without being detected, and she had seen no sign of a large man or even his shadow. She forced herself to lie there, to wait for some inkling of his proximity.

The wind carried the sounds of the night, of the mountainous terrain; the wind created its own accompaniment while Jeannine's pulse pounded in her temples. Perhaps he had gone back to the house . . . to finish off la señora? . . . Might he have gone in totally the wrong direction? Would he have been misled to some other part of the estate? Her hopes soared as she scanned the area, assessing her chances of reaching the open garage.

In the darting shadows of the waning night, everything seemed peacefully serene. There was nowhere he could be hiding that would be in her path to the escape of the car. Excitement built within her and she pulled herself up to a runner's crouch. Again she waited; again she scanned the area from this new vantage point.

Quiet. Only the wind . . . the loyal wind.

From some silent cue of her psyche, Jeannine sprinted forward with all the strength and speed she possessed. In moments she had reached the small car, thrown open the door, and turned the keys in the ignition. The engine, as always, turned over instantly, and she ground the gears getting into reverse, burned rubber in her haste to back out of the garage . . . and scant seconds later, Jeannine was driving madly through the winding curves down the mountainside.

When she was about halfway down the mountainside, Jeannine felt safe enough to pull over to the side of the road to pull herself together. She knew she'd probably go right off the road if she didn't calm down. Leaving the engine running, she rolled down the window and drew in a series of deep breaths of fresh night air, then rested her head against the seat. Slowly, she began to feel more at ease, her tensions — though still present — were more in control. She no longer felt like some panicked animal, some wounded fox victimized by human and hound alike, chased into a dark hole to shiver out its fate.

Breathing with a degree of normalcy, she began to feel the bruises and scratches she had incurred in her painful escape beneath the bushes. It was still too dark to make out the seriousness of her cuts, but she could make out the dark blotches of mud and blood mixed and caked on her arms and hands.

When she felt she had sufficiently gotten

her wits about her, Jeannine straightened up in the seat of the car, and out of habit glanced in the rearview mirror before putting the car in first gear.

Even as her eyes fell upon the mirror, a dark form rose up from the back seat. A large, hulking dark form of a man. The form moved slowly, very slowly, until it was seated upright behind her.

Jeannine fought the terror in her heart . . . the only word to escape her lips was "Miguel! . . ."

Chapter 19

"No, my dear, not Miguel," the man said in a deadly soft voice.

Jeannine involuntarily closed her eyes tightly, as if by so doing she could obliterate his presence. She knew the voice of her pursuer, she knew it well.

"I knew you'd head for the car. You had no choice, really."

"And you just waited for me," she said tonelessly, wondering why they were bothering to speak at all. Why didn't he just kill her as he intended to do anyway.

"Yes."

Jeannine's throat constricted painfully as she held back the tears she longed to release. "But why did you have to stab Doña Josefina! What has she done to you? Why is everyone so secretive about the hatred between you?"

"I didn't stab her, Jeannine," Dr. Franklin said. "I swear to you I didn't. She stabbed herself!"

"But why should she?" Jeannine demanded. In a strange sort of way, she was glad that they were talking after all. With the weeks and weeks of hints and evasions of lies and confusion, at least now she would learn the truth.

Dr. Franklin sighed heavily. "I had hoped to be able to scare you away, Jeannine. God knows, I did everything possible to get you to leave. But you wouldn't be frightened away. You stubbornly just wouldn't be scared off!"

Jeannine found herself growing strangely calm, as if she had found herself in the center of the hurricane and her worst fears were over. It was peaceful here; the frantic turmoil no longer tore at her. She was going to learn the truth — even if it killed her. Her fear now seemed a foolish, girlish thing; Dr. Franklin intended to murder her, but now it was not some nameless, faceless assailant without rhyme or reason. If he had truly wanted her dead, he could have done so on many previous occasions; there had to be some sense to his plan, he was not insane.

"Why did you want me to leave?" she asked levelly.

"I wanted to tell you, Jeannine, that day you came to my cottage. At that time, there was still some hope that I might have been able to get rid of John 'accidentally.' But when Miguel told me of Doña Josefina's plan for the two of them to leave 'Puerta de Paz' . . ."

"Miguel told you!"

"Yes," Dr. Franklin said, a tone of pride in his voice. "Miguel frequently came to visit me very late at night. He'd spend hours with me, talking to me, keeping me company until he'd have to return to the house. Until he'd go back to his great-grandmother to do her selfish bidding."

Jeannine was at a total loss for words.

"You see, my dear, Miguel is my son. My illegitimate son. That is the source of my feud with Doña Josefina. She has never forgiven me for it. It would have been bad enough just knowing of her granddaughter's infidelity to her husband, but when she died giving Miguel his life, well, I'm sure you can imagine the rest."

"Does Miguel know?" The moment she'd asked the question, she felt foolish.

"Of course he does! Not that Doña Josefina ever told him — but I did. I watched over that boy from the moment he was born. Watched him grow up, at a distance. Watched him go to school, at a distance. Miguel is my only child. I love him more than life itself. So, when I thought he was old enough to know the truth . . . I told him."

"And how old was old enough?" Jeannine asked, amazed at how Dr. Franklin's voice changed as he spoke of his only son.

"Fifteen."

Jeannine felt heartsick for Miguel. Fifteen! Such an impressionable age! What a horrible thing to have to learn at any time or from anyone . . . but to hear it from someone you consider almost a stranger? The town gossip?

"There was," Dr. Franklin continued, "a small scandal following Miguel's birth. We couldn't keep it a secret from everyone, and many of my patients drifted away to other doctors. Everyone likes to hear about gossip and scandal, my dear, but no one likes to have it affect his life directly. They just didn't trust a doctor who had become romantically involved with one of his patients."

Strangely, instead of fear Jeannine felt an enormous sympathy for the man. She didn't condone what he had done, but she could understand. The literature and casebooks of the world were filled with similar stories; moments of weakness, blinded by love — had she not herself been willing to love someone whom she thought might be a murderer? How could she censure Dr. Franklin? "But why couldn't you have told me this before? Why did you have to commit murder?"

"Dr. Sternig? I had no choice. I panicked, Jeannine. Human stupidity. I regret that far more than anything I've done. He came to see me after he left your house. He wasn't too sure of just how he knew that I was the one, but he had a strong hunch. Based on what he gleaned from Doña Josefina, and from you, he had deduced that I was the one responsible for the events at the house. I was totally unprepared for that possibility, or for his visit and his accusations. I just turned cold, panicked, and shot him. I hadn't meant to. I didn't even really want to. But I did it."

Jeannine could not help but hear the utter sincerity in the man's voice. She hated him for a moment; the loss of Dr. Sternig and the senseless stupidity of his death made her recoil from Dr. Franklin as if he were subhuman. But the reaction did not last. In its place came the realization that Dr. Franklin was, after all, a psychopath. She wasn't sure yet just what direction it took, but Jeannine was beginning to realize that, kindly and well-meaning as he otherwise was, in at least one area Dr. Franklin was deranged. It occurred to her, also, that she should be terrified for her own life — yet she was not.

241

Her senses were inexplicably alert, and the sound of the car's engine idling seemed to cast a spell over her; seemed to speak to her.

The dawn was beginning to break in the east, and now they could make out each other's features, see the expression upon each other's faces.

"I am very sorry that I must kill you, Jeannine. If only you'd taken the warnings . . . if only you'd gone away. . . ." He leaned forward slowly, patting her shoulder with one hand.

Jeannine could see that he had a silk scarf in his other hand which he was bringing closer to her throat. She glanced briefly at his face in the mirror, at the kindly smile, the saddened expression for what he believed he had to do. With a precision and dexterity she'd not believed herself capable of, Jeannine put the car into first gear, pressed down heavily on the gas pedal, and drove the car off the shoulder of the road, through the rough terrain, and the moment she made out the edge of the mountainside before them, she threw open the car door and jumped out.

The VW didn't have a back door.

Chapter 20

When Jeannine regained consciousness, she was in a hospital room with an IV connected to her arm; it felt rather like a mosquito bite. There was no disorientation as she awoke; no questioning of where she was, or of how she got there. Jeannine knew. She knew only too well. The evil at "Puerta de Paz" had been exposed.

She glanced around the sterile room, then at the shaded window which held back the glaring sunlight, then at her arms and hands. They were clean now, the mud had been removed, and she was happy to see that she was not as badly cut and bruised as she had initially feared. Her legs ached when she attempted to move them slightly, and the flesh felt as if it had been attacked by an army of razor blades. Her left ankle felt stiff and numb and it throbbed painfully; she realized, then, that it was in a firmly wrapped bandage and she hoped that it was merely sprained and not broken.

From what seemed a great distance, she heard the muted sounds of hospital life;

telephones that rang as if blocks away, wheeled stretchers rolling a rubbery path down linoleum floors, a buzzer that might have been from the floor above — yet she also knew that all of these sounds were just beyond her door. Her room smelled of gauze and antiseptic chemicals, but as her senses became more acute, she realized that she also was able to smell flowers. Painfully, she twisted her head toward the prim white bureau on the other side of the room; there sat a huge array of bright yellow and orange flowers looking very much like a Van Gogh painting. Though Jeannine ached incredibly, her mind was quite clear. She had leapt from the car as it had gone over the side of the mountain; she had deliberately driven the car off, and jumped out in time to save her own life. But what had happened to Dr. Franklin?

Her imagination was filled with scenes of a car hurtling, bursting into billowing smoke and flames, of Dr. Franklin screaming to get out, frantically pounding at the windows to escape the holocaust of his own grim death. Jeannine shuddered. She squeezed her eyes tightly shut, hoping to obliterate the images, but instead envisioned the charred car lying on its side, an unidentifiable Dr. Franklin a grotesque blackened human form. It was too horrible for her to endure.

Fortunately, Dr. Ortíz chose that moment to look in on her. "Ah, Jeannine, you're awake! Good, good!" he said, coming to her bedside and lifting her wrist to take her pulse. Even in his white hospital coat, he still looked like a banker; while he felt her pulse, the expression on his face could have been the same as that of a loan officer deciding whether or not someone was a good credit risk.

Jeannine was so pleased to see any human being at all, that she couldn't resist smiling despite the tape pulling on one side of her face. "Will I live?" she asked lightly.

"Oh, yes. Oh yes!" the doctor chortled. "It wasn't the lacerations so much, or even your fractured ankle from the fall . . . but all that excitement brought on a rather severe attack. In your weakened and highly emotional condition, I was mostly worried about that. But you're a young and healthy woman. With plenty of rest and good care, you'll be just fine in no time."

"Dr. Franklin?" she began hesitantly, almost afraid to hear the answer. "And Doña Josefina?"

Dr. Ortíz looked at her compassionately as he released her wrist. "Why not let Miguel explain it all to you instead of getting bits and pieces from me."

"Is he here?" she asked tremulously.

Dr. Ortíz's lips curled into a shy smile. "He's been a fixture in the corridor since the moment you were brought in. In fact, it was he who found you and phoned me." The doctor paused as if anything involving emotions or love was too embarrassing for him to discuss. "Would you like to see him?"

"Would I like . . ." her voice trailed off incredulously. Nothing could have filled her with deeper pleasure, greater reward, than the chance to see him, to touch him. For the first time since she had come to Carmel-by-the-Sea, Jeannine experienced a tingling thrill at the prospect of seeing Miguel, a vibrancy that coursed through her entire body at the thought of being near to him.

Dr. Ortíz nodded sagely, the awkward smile still on his lips, and stepped out of the room. Seconds later, Miguel entered. He poised at the foot of her bed as if uncertain of his reception, an expression of scowling concern etched upon his brow. He seemed to hover there with indecision.

Jeannine found herself blushing radiantly, her blood pounding in her veins as she gazed at his handsome dark face, so masculinely virile, and his blazing dark eyes, so like his great-grandmother's. He aroused such depths of emotion within her that she thought she might burst from the total love she felt for this incredible man. What agonies he must have suffered knowing that he was an illegitimate child; what needless torment about possible scandals that would grieve his beloved great-grandmother. She longed to reach out and touch him, to reassure him that this was not the turn of the century, that no one really cared about such things anymore. It was the measure of the man that mattered, and not his lineage or the certificate that legalized it.

What seemed like endless moments passed with neither of them saying a word, neither of them making a move. At last, unable to stand it for a second longer, Jeannine smiled at him. "I know, Miguel. I know all about it now. You don't have to keep any more secrets . . . you're free from that burden — at least with me."

Miguel's face softened, his eyes changing expression from intense uncertainty to immense relief. As if jolted into action, he seemed to cover the distance between them in one motion. Only for a fraction of a second, he poised above her, looking into her eyes with such tenderness and desire that Jeannine could hardly breathe from the excitement he created within her.

Then he leaned over and kissed her, long-ingly, deeply. When he broke the kiss, he covered her face and her ears with small kisses murmuring endearments she would never forget. "I love you, my darling Jean-nine . . . I've loved you so much I was afraid of anything that might take you away. I was such a fool, such a coward when the acci-dents began — I was ready to believe any-thing rather than let you get away from me."

"My darling," Jeannine whispered, feeling his warm lips against her throat, upon her cheek, and brushing at her eyelids. "I've loved you, too. I thought you resented me, thought you looked upon me as some kind of silly interloper."

"I was afraid of what you'd think if you found out about me, about Aaron being my real father. I was certain you'd leave 'Puerta de Paz' and I'd never see you again — or worse, that you'd run into John's arms. I couldn't have stood that — couldn't have stood to see him kiss you or put his arms around you. I think I would have killed him if he'd won you."

"Then why were you so remote with me, so distant and cold?"

Miguel sat on the edge of the bed, holding her hand in his, and smiled at her. "I couldn't let you go," he said softly, "but I didn't have the courage to tell you the truth. That was at first. Then, when the accidents began and still you stuck it out, I knew you'd never leave the hacienda unless Doña Josefina fired you. . . . I had hoped that by making things very uncomfortable for you, by being the brooding, moody, melodramatic neurotic, that you'd want to get away on your own, that you'd quit. I feared for your safety, darling, and I just didn't know any other way to handle it."

Jeannine reached up with her free arm and brought his head to her breast. "It's all over now, my love, all the secrets are out . . . we can be together now."

Miguel raised his head slowly, then sat up and looked at her with a questioning expression. "Perhaps I'd better explain the whole thing, Jeannine. You deserve to know the whole truth."

Jeannine tensed with his words; she knew what she was about to hear would not be pleasant. "Doña Josefina?" she asked softly.

Miguel smiled wanly. "She's on the critical list, but Dr. Ortíz has high hopes. She's a very stubborn, pigheaded woman. He says he's never seen anyone with such a will to live!"

Jeannine sighed heavily with relief. "Thank God!"

"You see," Miguel began, "unknown to me, my father had been blackmailing Doña Josefina for a number of years, threatening to tell everyone of my illegitimacy if she didn't pay him his bribe every month."

"How did you learn this?" Jeannine asked, her curiosity piqued.

"Doña Josefina told me this morning," he answered, grinning impishly at her as if he knew that forevermore he would be answering her questions about anything and everything.

"But you said she was on the critical list!"

"Yes," he agreed. "But there's nothing wrong with her voice! They have her sedated to keep her from getting out of bed and petitioning the other patients to join the conservationists' roll call. The day that woman cannot speak out in protest is the day I'll believe she hasn't long to live," he added, laughing at the mere thought that anything would ever cut down his great-grandmother.

"Anyhow," he resumed, "what I never knew was that Aaron Franklin lived in horrendous guilt about me, feared that I would not receive my share of the inheritance. He was convinced that Grandmother would give me a legal token to prevent my suing the estate . . . but that she had otherwise cut me out of the will. He would go to her late at night and they would rendezvous in the attic where John and I used to play as boys, and there they would argue about me. Naturally, I never knew that."

"But how did he get in? No one ever saw him coming or going."

"Side entrance," Miguel answered cryptically. "Or more accurately, there's a storage room beneath the kitchen and a door that leads from the garden at the side of the house into that room. From there, he simply had to tiptoe up to the attic."

"But why should Doña Josefina endure his visits, much less the arguments and the blackmail?"

"To avoid scandal, to keep things quiet — the usual reasons one endures such things. I'm certain she had no idea how deranged my father had become, how dangerous he could be."

Jeannine frowned slightly. "So, in order to be sure you'd get your full share, he wanted to kill John?"

"Partially. The other reason for the many attempts was to frighten you away. Doña Josefina only told me about this today . . .

and it is something you must think about very carefully."

"Yes, Dr. Franklin told me that he'd wanted to scare me off — but why, darling? Why was it so important?"

Miguel squeezed her hand lovingly before going into the explanation. "Well, it would appear that under the original Spanish land grant, which is how Doña Josefina has kept control of her estates, all heirs must be of pure Spanish blood. Not only the heirs, but also their spouses and progeny."

"You mean that everyone in your family has been forced to marry someone of Spanish extraction? What happens if, say, John were to marry an American of German and Irish extraction?"

Miguel shrugged. "According to the land grant terms, he would then forfeit his share. Olga and I would be the only ones eligible to inherit the estate, subject to Doña Josefina's wishes in the matter."

"Then she cannot just arbitrarily leave the estates to whomever she wishes?"

"No. It must be very difficult for you to understand, darling, but terms and conditions of wills and estates are frequently little more than exercises in eccentricity; and land grants, in those days, were not very different. It was, more or less, a way of repaying a favor or service."

"But I thought la señora said that the Spanish had encouraged intermarriage. . . ."

"Ah, yes, among the officers and troops, but not among the aristocracy or those chosen to oversee the governing of the New World. I've no idea what the ancestor of Ignacio was like, but apparently, the Spanish throne had no wish to trust these lands to descendants who were not loyal to Spain. You have to remember that when these grants were being issued, no one had anticipated a United States of America would evolve. It was assumed that Spain would always own and control this part of the Americas. The grant was worded in such a way to insure the purity of the ruling class, and to reclaim the land for Spain if anyone defied its terms and wishes."

"That seems a strange way to go about it, though."

"Perhaps, but you'd be surprised at how many old California families have kept the line pure . . . whether for similar reasons or sheer chauvinism, I don't know."

Jeannine thought about what Miguel had said, letting it settle in her mind before speaking. She couldn't help marveling at the lengths to which the Old World ventured in their machinations of supremacy. "In other words, if it were known that Dr. Franklin was your father, you'd not be able to inherit your share of the estate?"

"Precisely."

"But what would happen if there were no pure Spanish-blooded heirs to inherit the lands?"

Miguel laughed. "I've not seen the actual grant, but I am rather confident that California would *not* give it back to Spain! I'm sure that it's merely a courtesy arrangement, and if there are no heirs, the lands would return to the State."

"But that is medieval," Jeannine protested, ignoring Miguel's amused expression. "You not only have to be a direct heir by descent, but you have to be of pure blood and Doña Josefina cannot dispose of her own property in any way she wishes, and, and . . ."

Miguel leaned forward and softly kissed her on the lips to silence her. "I've seen stranger situations than this one," he told her.

Jeannine took a deep breath and exhaled in exasperation. "All right, but then why would your father threaten to expose the truth . . . that would have been defeating his purpose!"

"You forget," Miguel said softly, ruefully, "my father was obsessed, his mind was not working in a logical manner. His obsession came to control him, to rule his every waking moment. In any other area, he was a good and rational man. But when it came to me or my inheritance or, for that matter, his blackmailing of Doña Josefina — which was all connected in his head — then something seemed to go askew in his thinking."

"And you never sensed this?" she asked as gently as she possibly could.

Miguel shook his head regretfully. "He would sometimes speak of the wonderful things I might do when I came into my share of the inheritance, but he never seemed rabid about it, never became incensed or flailed his arms like some maniac. I had no way of knowing," Miguel said, a note of self-accusation in his voice, as if he'd let everyone down by not reading his father's mind.

Jeannine thought about Miguel's words, about what he had revealed to her: the estate, the clause for the heirs, all of it. She also wondered how likely it was that Miguel would never have sensed his father's tunnel-visioned view of Miguel's inheritance. She glanced up at Miguel's face; scrutinized him as he stared at his hands, his thoughts known only to himself. And Jeannine's heart melted at the sight of his inner flagellation. "Darling," she said, "you mustn't blame yourself. The only way you might have known what Dr. Franklin was thinking was if you'd been *looking* for some symptom, some indication of his insanity. But there was no reason to. I knew him briefly, but I trusted him completely — even when la señora asked me to stay away from him, I still took his side. There was nothing about your father that even hinted that his mind might not be all right."

His hands slowly relaxed and he nodded. "Frankly, it wasn't until you came on the scene that he was motivated to do anything criminally insane. Naturally, he wanted to know what I thought of you very early on, and I told him the truth, told him I thought I was falling in love with you. So you see, in a way, I am responsible for tripping the lever of his greatest fear. Even if it were never known that he was my father, if I married you I would be forfeiting my share of the inheritance."

Heedless of the tube connected to her arm, Jeannine sat up and put her arms around Miguel's warm strong neck. "You can't punish yourself, darling. Should I go through life believing that I am responsible for Dr. Sternig's death?"

"No, of course not," he answered. "Dr. Sternig knew he was taking a chance going to see my father, he already suspected him. Did you know that he telephoned me in Monterey just before he went to Father's cottage? He asked me many leading questions . . . and it was then that I realized who was behind all the events at the hacienda. Or, at least, it began to formulate in the back of my mind. Then, when the newspaper told of Dr. Sternig's death . . . I knew."

"Then why didn't you come down sooner?" Jeannine asked, perplexed by the delay.

Miguel shrugged. "I'd worked late at the office. I didn't even see the paper until after midnight. As soon as I read about it, I drove down to my father's cottage to confront him. When he wasn't there, I put two and two together and immediately left for 'Puerta de Paz.' I saw the Volkswagen go over the side of the cliff; saw your body falling from the car . . . my God! I'll never forget it!"

"My poor darling," Jeannine mouthed against his ear. Hesitantly, afraid of the answer, she asked, "And your father?"

He was very still for a moment, hardly even breathing. "He lived long enough for

Officer Shroyer to get a full confession out of him . . . at least, a full confession about the murder attempts — including yours. I strongly doubt there'll even be an inquiry as far as you're concerned."

"But he didn't reveal the truth about you? Even when dying, he was still trying to protect you?"

"Yes."

Jeannine's eyes brimmed with tears. "You must always remember only the goodness in him, Miguel. Fear and guilt twisted his mind, but he was not truly an evil man . . . The woman he loved died giving you birth, and the moment you were born — because he was your father — you were destined to lose your rightful share of a considerable estate. His guilt acted as a mental corkscrew wherever you were concerned."

"I suppose," Miguel answered quietly.

"But it's all over now, darling. It's all in the past."

Miguel looked at her, his love for her shining through his eyes. "And you don't mind that I'll never own 'Puerta de Paz'?"

Jeannine had to laugh at such a silly question. "I'm in love with you, Miguel de Lorca — not a house."

"Manuel!" la señora shouted through the

open door of her bedroom as the wiry man began to enter with a tray and three sherry glasses. "Get rid of all these awful flowers and plants! They make me feel as if I were already dead!"

"Sí, señora," Manuel replied, serving both Jeannine and Miguel before placing Doña Josefina's glass on the bedside table.

"It's an affront, that's what it is," she carried on. "Cutting flowers is to kill them! Why are humans such barbarians!"

Manuel winked at Miguel while he was facing away from la señora, signaling that she was certainly getting back to her old self. And Jeannine and Miguel exchanged glances of intimate affection, and amusement with Doña Josefina.

"Well," Miguel said, raising his glass in a toast, "Here's to you and 'Puerta de Paz' — may it live up to its name."

"*Salud y pesetas,*" Jeannine said, trying desperately to remember the correct pronunciation, which Miguel had coached her in the night before.

La señora nodded slowly, lovingly at Miguel. "You have already begun to teach her Spanish? You're not even married two weeks yet, and so soon you are the dominating tyrant?"

"I want to learn!" Jeannine exclaimed. "I

asked him to teach me something appropriate!"

"Then he should have taught you the balance of the toast, *niña*. '*Y el tiempo para gastarlas.*' A woman of my age cannot be certain that she'll have the time to enjoy her health and her money!"

"Well," Miguel laughed, "if you'll stop trying to kill yourself . . ."

"Don't be impudent, Miguel," la señora chided. "I had very little choice. Besides, it was the only way I could think of to try to stop your father's insane plan. If I were dead, he wouldn't have dared attempt to kill either Juanillo or Jeannine. Alive, I gave him a motive; dead, he was defeated."

"But surely you didn't really plan to kill yourself?" Jeannine asked horrified.

La señora brought her brilliant dark eyes to rest on the young girl, a gleeful little smile playing on her lips. "If, and when, I decide it is time for me to die, my child, you may rest assured that I shall not bungle it. If there's anything I cannot stand it's inefficiency!"

Jeannine and Miguel laughed heartily, and even la señora couldn't resist a chuckle at herself and her defiance of any power stronger than her own will. "On the other hand," she said, her face resuming its austere mask, "I wouldn't put off having children for any undue length of time. If you expect them to have a doting great-great-grandmother, I would recommend prudent haste."

Miguel put his arms around Jeannine and, leaning over la señora, asked her in a stage whisper, "Just how old are you, *abuelita?*"

La señora slapped him lightly on the cheek. "Old enough to know that babies are not made by asking old women foolish questions!"